Ada Cambridge

# A MERE CHANCE

Volume III

Ada Cambridge

**A MERE CHANCE**
*Volume III*

ISBN/EAN: 9783741123375

Manufactured in Europe, USA, Canada, Australia, Japa

Cover: Foto ©Andreas Hilbeck / pixelio.de

Manufactured and distributed by brebook publishing software
(www.brebook.com)

Ada Cambridge

**A MERE CHANCE**

# A NOVEL.

BY

## ADA CAMBRIDGE,

AUTHOR OF "IN TWO YEARS TIME," &c.

IN THREE VOLUMES.

### VOL. III.

LONDON:

## RICHARD BENTLEY AND SON,

Publishers in Ordinary to Her Majesty the Queen,

NEW BURLINGTON STREET.

1882.

# CONTENTS

OF

# THE THIRD VOLUME.

# A MERE CHANCE.

## CHAPTER I.

### A PARABLE.

IT was about a month after the foregoing conversation took place, that Melbourne society was fluttered by a rumour that the engagement between Mr. Kingston and Miss Fetherstonhaugh, which had been unaccountably broken off, was "on" again, and that the long-delayed wedding was to take place immediately. Rumour for once in the way, was perfectly correct.

People went to call at Toorak, and found the aunt serene and radiant, and the bride-elect wearing all the honours of her position—not shyly as of yore, but with a quiet candour and dignified self-possession that was not generally considered becoming under the circumstances.

It was thought that a little humility would be proper in a young person who was going to enjoy such altogether undeserved good fortune.

It happened while she was staying at South Yarra. *How* it happened nobody quite knew. Gossip attributed it to Mrs. Reade's manœuvres; but Mrs. Reade, far from encouraging anything of the sort, set herself steadily against it, and warned Mr. Kingston of probable consequences in the most terse and trenchant manner (she had taken a very different view of the situation since her return from Adelonga).

Gossip likewise attributed it to the seductions of the new house, which was beginning to shadow forth in Palladio-gingerbread of the most ambitious pattern, the magnificence of the establishment that was to be; but gossip was equally misinformed in this respect.

Rachel was as ready as ever to admire the house, and the beautiful tiles, and carvings, and hangings, and upholstery, that were constantly being designed and produced for its adornment; she fully understood how much they represented for whoever was to possess and enjoy them. But they had not a feather-weight of value in her eyes as compared

with the happiness she had hoped for
and lost; they did not suggest the idea
of compensation or consolation in even
a slight degree. The fact was that
Mr. Kingston was determined to have her.

Of late he had seemed—not to Rachel,
but to Mrs. Reade—to have a sort of
half-sullen doggedness in his determina-
tion, indicating that he was as much bent
upon winning the game as upon winning
the stakes—that he meant, before all
things, not to be beaten in the enterprise
upon which he had set his heart.

And in this frame of mind he waited
upon opportunity; and in the end, opportunity, as so often happens in such
cases, served him.

One day Beatrice and her husband
went out of town to lunch, and Rachel
had a long, lonely afternoon. It came

on to rain, and it was grey and chilly. Dull weather always sent her spirits down several degrees below the normal temperature, and just now she was morbidly sensitive to its influence. If Beatrice had been at home there would have been a fire in no time, summer though it was; in her absence Rachel did not like to take upon herself to order one. She lay on a sofa with a shawl over her feet, and listened to the rain pattering on the window, and felt cold, and dismal, and deserted.

At five o'clock she was pining for her tea, and thinking it had been forgotten, rang for it; and the smart young parlour-maid, interrupted in an interesting *tête-à-tête* with the next door coachman, and blessed with few opportunities for the indulgence of a naturally restive temper, brought it in with a protesting *nonchalance*, a teapotful of nasty liquid, made with water that had not boiled, and a couple of slices of bread and butter that would have charmed a hungry schoolboy--such as would never have been presented to the mistress of the house, as Rachel well knew.

This small indignity, so very small as it was, greatly aggravated the vague sense of desolation and orphanhood—the feeling that she was a person of no consequence to anybody—which possessed her just now. And while she was in the lowest depths of despondency, in the deepest indigo of blues, Mr. Kingston calling, discovered her solitude and came in, tenderly deferential, full of solicitude for her health and comfort, stooping from his higher sphere of social im-

portance to pay homage to her still in
her forlorn insignificance.

For the space of half-an-hour perhaps
she felt that it would be good to be
married to somebody—to anybody—who
would love and take care of her, and
make the servants treat her with proper
respect ; and a mere chance enabled Mr.
Kingston to take advantage of that accident.

Looking back afterwards she never
could understand how it was that she
had felt disposed to re-accept him ; but
the causes were as distinct as causes
usually are. Badly-made tea, and the
want of a fire in dull weather are,
amongst the multifarious factors of
human destiny, greatly underrated.

Having said the fatal " yes "—or,
rather, having failed at the proper
moment to say " no," which Mr. Kingston

justly took to mean the same thing—
Rachel was allowed no more opportunities
for what her aunt called "shilly-shallying."

The day of the marriage was fixed
at once, and the preparations for her
trousseau simultaneously set on foot.

The girl had hardly come to realise
the extraordinary thing that she had
done when she found herself being
measured for all sorts of wearing apparel,
and consulted about the arrangements
for her honeymoon tour. Then she set
herself to do her duty in the state of life
to which she imagined herself "called,"
with a kind of hopeless resignation. She
recognised the fact that this second
mistake was not revocable like the first ;
and therefore she understood that it was
not to be considered a mistake.

All her life and energy now had to

be dedicated to the task of making it justifiable to her own conscience and in the eyes of all men.

And so she was sweet and gentle to her affianced husband, promising him that, though she could not love him first and best, if he was content to have her as she was (and he assured her he was quite content), she would do all in her power to prove herself a good and true wife to him; and she was tractable and obedient in the hands of her aunt, and ready to fall in with all the arrangements that were made for her.

But, as the wedding-day drew near, the dread of it showed itself to Mrs. Reade, if to no one else, in the dumb eloquence of the sensitive, truth-telling face. That little person who had such a talent for managing, stood aside at

this crisis, and did not intermeddle with
the strange course of events.

In none of the affairs that she had
promoted and directed and brought to
successful terminations, had she taken
such a deep and painful interest as
she now felt in this, which she had been
powerless to control; but, for the first
time in her life, she was afraid to speak
to her young cousin of the thoughts
that both their minds were full of,
lest she might be called upon to advise
where she found it was impossible to
decide what was for the best, and only
waited helplessly upon Fate, like an
ordinary incapable woman.

On the night before the wedding—a
soft, bright, early autumn night—
Rachel gave her a distinct intimation
if she had wanted it, that the marriage

however it might turn out eventually,
was by no means undertaken as marriages should be.

The girl stole away from the drawing-
room while the others were temporarily
absorbed in the preparations that were
going on for the great ceremonial, and
Mrs. Reade, hunting for her anxiously,
found her standing in the moonlight
by the kitchen-garden gate.

"Looking at that house again!" the
little woman exclaimed. "Why, you
must know every stick and stone by
heart. I never miss you that I don't
find you here."

"I am like our poor Jenny and the
tank," said Rachel, gazing still at the
imposing pile before her, sharply black
and white against the soft light of the sky.

"Who is Jenny, may I ask?"

"A dear cat we used to have. She fell into a deep tank one day when father and I were not at home, and for two days she was struggling at the edge of the water clinging to a bit of brickwork, and no one came to help her. Some men heard her cries, but did not know where she was. As soon as we came home, of course I found it all out; and I got a large bough of wattle and lowered it down, and so she was saved when she was very nearly gone. Oh, poor thing, what a state she was in! I sat up with her all night. But she never got over it. She was not exactly mad, but she was never in her right mind afterwards."

"Well?" said Mrs. Reade who was greatly mystified. "I can't see the drift of your allegory so far."

"No; I was going to tell you. Ever after this happened, we had to keep a constant watch upon her to prevent her from throwing herself into the tank again. If she heard the sound of the lid being moved, she would rush to it in a sort of frenzy. A bricklayer was doing something to it one day, and we had to lock her up, she was in such a frantic state. She would be gentle and quiet at other times, but as soon as she thought the lid was being opened, she got quite mad to go to it. And at last a new servant, who did not know of this, left the lid off one day, and poor Jenny seized her chance, and jumped in and drowned herself."

"And that is your well, you mean?" said Mrs. Reade, pointing to the house.

"And you are immolating yourself, like

Jenny? Oh, Rachel, what are you talking about !"

"I am talking nonsense, I know," said Rachel, with an impressive air of artificial composure; "but somehow Jenny happened to come into my head. Beatrice, do you know I have been thinking of something."

"Of what? Oh, dear me, I wish to goodness you would think like a sensible girl, who knew her own mind sometimes."

"I have been thinking what I ought to do. I ought to just put on my hat and jacket and run away. I could go to a friend, a poor widow, who used to be very kind to me in the old days, and she would let me stay with her until I could get a situation. No, don't scold me—it is ten o'clock, isn't it? It is

too late for a girl to be out at night
alone. I *can't* do it, if I would."

"And would you, indeed if you could?"
demanded Mrs. Reade, holding her by
her wrists and looking imploringly into
her face. "Do you really mean that
you have a mind to do such a thing,
Rachel?"

Rachel was silent for a few seconds
and then she began to cry bitterly.

"Oh, I don't know—I don't know!"
she said, turning her head wildly from
side to side. "Sometimes I feel one
way and sometimes another. I want
somebody—somebody strong, like Roden
—to tell me what it is right to do!"

For a moment Mrs. Reade weighed
the merits of the proposition, and all
that lay against it, with as near an approach to impartial judgment as true

friendship and human fallibility allowed.
And the thought of Rachel's weakness
of purpose and inability to take care of
herself, and of Mr. Dalrymple's tra-
dittional character, turned the scale.

"You cannot go back *now*," she said.
"My darling, you have doubly given
yourself to Mr. Kingston, and you must
try to make yourself happy with him—
much can be done by trying, if you will
only make up your mind !"

It was the last chance that Rachel
had, and she accepted the fate that
deprived her of it with characteristic
meekness.

"Yes, I will try," she said, wiping
her eyes. " It is too late to go back now."

## CHAPTER II.

### "WHEN YULE IS COLD."

RACHEL, when she did at last get married, had a very stately wedding, if that was any comfort to her. The weather was beautiful, to begin with ; a lovelier autumn morning even Australia could not have furnished, to be an omen of good luck for the future years.

Each of the eight young Melbourne

belles who had been invited to assist
at the interesting ceremony took
care to point out the significance
of sunshine and a cloudless sky
when offering their congratulations
to the bride and to the bridegroom
also.

The bridegroom on this occasion
by no means filled the humble office
which tradition and custom assigned
to him. There was not a bridesmaid
of them all who did not feel that she
was much more Mr. Kingston's bridesmaid than Mrs. Kingston's.

Not only were they better acquainted
and on more friendly terms generally
with him than with her, but he had
far more to say to them, and practically far more to do with them,
in the course of the day and in the

discharge of his and their official
duties.

He was the prince of bridegrooms,
indeed. He had made magnificent
settlements upon his wife (though the
credit of that really belonged to Mr.
Hardy, who, for once in a way, had
to be reckoned with in the progress of
these arrangements) ; and his wedding
presents were on an equally noble
scale.

The bridesmaids' bracelets were solid
evidences of his worth in every sense
of the term, and inasmuch as each
bracelet slightly differed from the rest,
though all were equally costly, of the
excellence of his taste and tact. They
were valued thereafter by their respec-
tive recipients rather as parting
keepsakes from their bachelor friend

than as mementoes of his auspicious marriage.

And the diamond necklace that was his special wedding-day gift to his bride, and which lay just under the ruffled lace encircling her white throat —a dazzling ring of shifting lights and colours—a magnet to the eyes of all spectators—was worthy to have been a gift from Solomon to the Queen of Sheba.

There was not a servant in the house, nor near it, who did not receive some token of the princely fashion in which he improved this great occasion, and who did not participate in the general impression that he more than rivalled, in popularity and importance, the beautiful young lady whom he had won.

Of the company, all were charmed
with his gaiety, his affability, and his
delightful *sang-froid.* He was never
for a moment embarrassed. He overflowed with airy courtesies, not only
to his bride, but to all her maids and
friends.

He made a brilliant speech, that
exactly hit the happy medium between
tearful pathos and unfeeling jocularity,
and that was full of well-bred witti-
cisms, provocative of gentle, well-
bred laughter. He was, in short, all
that a bridegroom ought to be, and
so very seldom is. He covered himself
with honour.

Rachel, on the contrary, seemed to
have been mesmerised into temporary
lifelessness. It was expected that she
would be shy and fluttered, and bathed

in blushes ; but she was not agitated
at all, and she did not blush at all.
She bore herself generally with a
statuesque composure that was thought
by some to be very dignified, and by
others very wooden and stupid, and
that was a little depressing to witness
from either point of view. From the
beginning of the day she wore this
unnatural calmness.

Mrs. Reade had been in terror lest
she should give way to unbecoming
excitement at some stage of the ceremonies, and was prepared to combat
the first symptoms of hysteria with such
material and moral remedies as were
most likely to be efficacious.

She had strictly enjoined Lucilla,
who had brought the baby to the
wedding, not to let that irresistible

child appear upon any account, and bidden her restrict herself to the most perfunctory caresses until the public ordeal was over. But long ere this point was reached the little woman was longing to see some signs of the emotional weakness that she had deprecated, and there were none.

The bride was as beautiful as a sculptor's ideal, but as cold as the marble which dimly embodies it. She had apparently nerved herself for a sacrificial rite, or else the greatness of her suffering had numbed her; or she was calm with resignation and despair.

"I wish," said Mrs. Reade to herself, in the middle of the marriage service, "I wish I had stopped it last night. I have made a mistake."

But as this thought occurred to her, she was standing—a splendid little figure in ruby velvet and antique lace —in the midst of scores of other splendid figures, a helpless witness to the irrevocable consummation of her mistake, which after all was less hers than anybody's.

Rachel had given her "troth" to her husband, and he was putting the ring that was the sign and seal of it—the token and pledge of the solemn vow and covenant betwixt them made—upon her finger.

When the breakfast was over, that domestic pendant to the religious ceremony having "gone off" with great success, Mrs. Kingston, in due course, retired to put on her travelling dress.

The bridesmaids proper were dispensed with at this stage, and the two married cousins went upstairs with the bride.

It was Beatrice now who was tender and caressing; Lucilla, who did not see very far below the surface of anything, and was delighted with the pomp and circumstance of this new alliance in the family, and charmed, like all happy matrons, to welcome a new comer into the matrimonial ranks, overflowed with unwonted gaiety.

" Now we are *all* married !" she exclaimed, sinking upon a sofa in Rachel's room, and looking very fair and young—as if marriage had thoroughly agreed with her—in a pale blue French dress of the highest fashion. " And we have all married so well, haven't we? And we have all got such good husbands. Oh, how nice it will be when Rachel and Laura come back and begin housekeeping! John is going to let me have a house in town, too, as soon as Isabel and Bruce come home, so that we shall be down for part of the year; and then what a cosy little family circle we shall make! But Rachel will be at the head of us all. Ah, dear child, you will know now how nice it is to be a married woman —to have your own husband with you always — such a delightful, attentive husband, too, as I know he will be— and your own home—such a beautiful home——"

"You lock up her diamonds, Lucilla," Mrs. Reade interrupted, handing the starry necklace to her sister. " And,

Rachel, dear, don't stand and tire
yourself. Sit down, and let me dress
you."

Rachel, when her bridal lace and
satin had been taken off, sat down to
be sponged and brushed, and to have
her travelling boots laced up.

Beatrice performed her lady's-maid
offices in silence, while Lucilla handed
her what she wanted, and pleasantly
chatted on ; and when all was done,
and the bride, in russet homespun, was
ready for her departure, there were a
few words whispered that Mrs. Thornley
did not . hear.

"My darling, you *said* you would try."

"Yes, Beatrice, dear ; yes, I am
trying."

"You are not finding it very hard—
too hard—are you."

" It will be easier in a little while."

" If you make an effort, Rachel—if you make up your mind—if you are kind and good to your husband, and try to keep him straight, and to make his home happy——"

" Yes, dear; yes. I am going to do all I can. But to-day I can only feel that I have lost—*quite* lost—Roden. I feel now as if he were dead. Even the memory of him I must not comfort myself with any more. That is what I feel hard. But I am trying to get over it. I have promised Mr. Kingston —Graham—all those solemn promises, and I *must* keep them—I will. It is only at first that I don't know how to bear it; but it will be easier by-and-bye. We must not talk about it,

Beatrice; it is wrong to talk about it
now. And, oh! I do so dread that I
shall break down."

She did break down at last. When
she descended the staircase into the
hall she found all the company awaiting
her, the front door open, and the carriage
that was to take her away being packed
with her travelling bags and wraps.

She shook hands with all the guests,
and smiled a gentle response to their
congratulatory farewells; she shook
hands with John and his fellow-
servants; she kissed her uncle and
thanked him for all his kindness to
her; she embraced Lucilla and Beatrice
with silent fervour, and then her stately
aunt, to whom she repeated her grateful
acknowledgements for the home and care
that had been given her."

"I am afraid I have not made much return to you for your goodness to me, dear Aunt Elizabeth," she said, with pathetic earnestness, but with no agitation of voice or manner.

To her intense surprise the majestic woman suddenly burst into tears.

"Oh, my child!" she said, tenderly, "I hope I have been as good an aunt to you as you have been a good niece to me. I hope you will be very, very happy, my darling. If you are not, I shall never forgive myself."

Mr. Kingston, of course, was standing by, and a frown fell like a cloud over his face. Mrs. Reade was also standing by, and she looked at him steadily for a few seconds with clear, bright eyes.

"Come, Rachel," he said, and he only

looked at his wife; "we shall lose our train if we don't make haste."

Rachel withdrew herself from her aunt's arms, and Mr. Kingston took her by the hand and led her away, followed from the house to her carriage by all her train. She was a good deal shaken by the little incident that had so unexpectedly occurred.

There was no mystery to her in what Mrs. Hardy had said, but the thing she had done was very strange aud very touching. It invested the Toorak House and all its belongings with a new charm that the orphan girl had never felt before with all the kindness that she had enjoyed there.

At no time in the fourteen or fifteen months that she had lived in it had it seemed so much her "home" as at

this moment, when her aunt cried like
a mother at parting from her—so de-
sirable a place to stay in now that she
had to go.

"Well," said Mr. Kingston, when the
carriage was fairly out of the Hardy
grounds, and he had waved a gracious
adieu with the tips of his fingers to
the woman at the lodge, who stood in
her Sunday best and white satin cap-
ribbons, smiling and curtseying, to see
them pass; "well, that is a good thing
over, isn't it? Of all the senseless in-
stitutions of this world, a wedding *à la
mode* is about the most preposterous.
You look knocked up already, when
you ought to be fresh for your
travels."

He spoke with a little nervous irritation, and Rachel did not answer

him. Her heart was beating very fast, beating in her ears and in her throat, as well as in the place where its active operations were usually carried on.

All her powers were concentrated upon a desperate effort to postpone that breaking-down which she had dreaded, and which she felt was inevitable, until she could shut herself within four walls again. But she could not postpone it.

Her husband took her hand and asked her what was the matter with her—whether she felt ill, or whether she was regretting after all that she had married him; whether she was going to make him happy, as she had promised, or to curse his life with its bitterest disappointment—speaking half

in love, half in anger, with a sudden
outburst of protesting entreaty pro-
voked by her irresponsive silence. And
she began to cry—almost to scream—
in the most violent and alarming
manner.

"My dear love! my sweet child!"
cried the bridegroom, aghast. "I did
not mean to vex you, Rachel. I did not
mean to blame you, my pet. Rachel,
Rachel, hush! do hush! Don't let that
confounded coachman go back and say
— Rachel, do you hear?" — giving
her a little shake—"there are people
passing. For Heaven's sake don't make
a scene in the street, whatever you
do!"

Rachel was almost beside herself with
excitement, but she was awake to the
indecency of betraying her emotion to

the servants and the passers-by. More-
over, something in her husband's voice
steadied her.

By a strong effort she checked the
headlong impulse to rave and scream
that for a few seconds was almost
overpowering, and held herself in with
shut teeth and tight-locked hands, wildly
sobbing under her breath, and by-and
bye, when the first rush of passion had
spent itself, she became quiet and tractable, fortunately, before they reached the
railway-station.

Mr. Kingston was terribly shocked
and outraged by this behaviour. He
would have given anything to be able
to scold her—in a gentle and judicious
manner, of course—but he was afraid
to attempt such a thing, or even to
speak of the probable causes that

had led to such deplorable impropriety.

He rummaged for his spirit-flask, and
made her drink a few drops of brandy,
which nearly choked her; he found
some eau-de-Cologne and bathed her
face; he got her to put on a thicker
veil, which happened to be amongst
the luxuries that her aunt and cousins
had stuffed into her travelling-bag;
and he kissed her and petted her, and
when she attempted to explain and
excuse herself, bade her "Hush! till
another time," and would not listen to her.

His immediate anxiety was to restore
her personal appearance and her powers
of self-command. The more important
matters could wait. And he succeeded
in his efforts; she did not break down
any more.

Their journey that day was not very
far. An hour or two in the train, and
then half a dozen miles in a comfortable covered buggy, and they reached
the country house which had been
placed at their disposal—the best sub-
stitute to be had for that charming
residence on the shores of the bay at
Sydney—where they were to spend two
or three weeks in their own society
before starting by the next mail to
Europe.

As they were driving through the
silent bush, in the dusk of that
autumn day, and the bridegroom,
wrapped in his fur-collared overcoat,
was musing not very happily upon
the success that had crowned his long-
cherished hopes and plans, his young
wife slipped her hand under his arm,

and laid her cheek upon his coat-sleeve.

"Graham," she whispered softly.

He turned round quickly, and took her in his arms. It was the first time she had spoken his name and offered him a caress voluntarily, and he was greatly touched and cheered.

"Will you forgive me?" she said, not shrinking away from his embrace, but creeping into it as she had never done before. "And, oh, will you love me, in spite of it all?"

"Love you!" he echoed, tenderly. "My sweet, I have always loved you more than anybody in the world, and I always shall. It will not be on *my* side that love will be wanting."

She said no more, but she lay still, with her head in its soft little sealskin cap on his breast, as if she liked to feel his arms about her.

It was so new to him, and so immeasurably delightful. He had never expected to feel happier (even on his wedding day) than he felt now, with his best beloved, who had been so impracticable, his own at last, giving herself up to him in this way.

Poor, parasitic little heart, full of spreading tendrils! It was essential to its very existence that it should have *something* to cling to—which was a view of the case, that happily did not chance to strike him.

# CHAPTER III.

### A DISCOVERY.

THERE was a great ball at Toorak on the night of the wedding, and like all the nuptial ceremonies, it went off with great *éclat*.

Mrs. Hardy recovered her serenity very quickly after the bride's departure, and appeared in the evening, clothed in smiles and sapphire velvet, looking the proud woman that it was generally conceded she had a right to be. Lucilla, at home for the first time since her sister Laura's wedding, and since her accession to the dignities of maternity, and carrying herself very prettily as a personage of consequence amongst the unmarried friends of her girlhood, looked extremely well and very happy, and reflected great honour upon her family in a variety of ways. Beatrice also was unusually brilliant, not only in her personal appearance, but in her mode of discharging the duties of the occasion —a little too much so, indeed, if anything.

Some elderly ladies, and a very few young men, were subsequently heard to express an opinion that she carried that sharp and satirical manner of hers to an excess that was unbecoming in a person of her sex and years, even if she had married money and become a leader of fashion.

A little after midnight, these two young women, the one for the sake of her baby, and the other on account of her husband, excused themselves from further attendance on Mrs. Hardy, and drove back to South Yarra, where the Thornleys were staying, carrying their willing lords along with them.

When they reached home, where of course they found bright fires ready for them, the men retired to the smoking-room, Mrs. Reade having laid upon her brother-in-law the responsibility of keeping his host from getting "any worse than he was already;" and the ladies went upstairs to Lucilla's apartment.

Lucilla having only arrived in town the day before, she and her sister had

had no opportunity for what they called a good talk; and now the baby being found asleep and in his nurse's charge for the night, they sat down to begin it, having previously got rid of ball-room finery and made themselves comfortable in their dressing-gowns.

"Does Ned often get—a—like this?" Mrs. Thornley began, with a compassionate inflection in her soft voice. She knew of course that one couldn't expect everything, but still she was sorry that her sister's excellent marriage should have this particular drawback, than which she could hardly imagine one more unpleasant and embarrassing, and that a nice fellow like Ned, with a noble pedigree and the sweetest temper in the world, should take his social pleasures as a shearer would celebrate pay-day.

Mrs. Reade was thinking, at the same moment, that John was ageing very fast and getting immensely stout, and that his manner of addressing his wife, and his bearing towards her generally, was more peremptory and dictatorial than *she* would feel inclined to put up with if she were in Lucilla's place.

"Oh, no," said the little woman, sharply; "it is only on these festive occasions, when I am not able to look after him properly. And at the worst he is not very bad. He never gets obstinate and quarrelsome, as some men do—only vaguely argumentative and subsequently sleepy. I should think no husband, with so pronounced a tendency that way could be easier to manage—if one knows how to manage."

"You were always a splendid manager, Beatrice."

"Well, I just hold him well in hand —that's all. I know he can't help it, to a certain extent, so I don't keep always worrying at him about it. It is only now and then that I give him a real good talking to—to prevent his thinking I might grow indifferent, as much as anything."

"He is such a dear, good fellow," said Lucilla, "but for that."

"He is a dear, good fellow, in spite of that," replied Beatrice, who allowed no one but herself to disparage her husband. "He is better worth having, with all his faults—and that is about the only one he has—than most of your brilliant society men. I only hope Mr. Kingston will be as little trouble to

Rachel as Ned has been to me—and half as good and kind to her."

"Yes, dear. I didn't mean to say that he wasn't the best of husbands— far from it. Indeed, we may both be thankful for our good luck in that respect—all of us, I should say. I should think no four girls in one family are more happily situated than we are."

"I hope so," sighed Mrs. Reade. "I hope we are all as happy as—as we are well off otherwise."

"Dear little Rachel!" said Mrs. Thornley, musingly. "I don't think there is any doubt about her being happy. It is quite extraordinary to see how fond of her Mr. Kingston is—*really* fond of her, I mean. Did you think he would ever marry such a young girl, Beatrice? and be so terribly anxious to

do it, too? I didn't. I suppose it was
her beauty captivated him."

" No," said Beatrice; "it was the
fact that she didn't want to captivate
him. That has been her charm all along
—he has felt that his honour was concerned in making her, and it has been
a difficult task."

"Oh, but I know he thinks a great
deal about beauty, and she is really the
prettiest girl in Melbourne, I do think,
though she does belong to us. She did
not look so pretty to-day though, as
I expected she would. That dead-white
in the morning that brides have to wear
does spoil even the best complexion. I
thought hers could stand anything, but
it can't stand that. When she wears
it in the evening, now—not dead-white,
but transparent white—she is a perfect

picture. At that ball of ours last year everybody was talking of her. She was in Indian muslin. John said she was like a wood anemone."

Mrs. Reade was gazing thoughtfully into the fire. The mention of the ball at Adelonga stirred many troubled thoughts. The real importance of that event, in its effect upon Rachel, had never been known to Mrs. Thornley, who was led to suppose that the suspension of Mr. Kingston's engagement in October was solely due to certain laxities on his part, which the girl would not condone.

Mrs. Hardy's terror lest " people" should get to know that a member of her family had had any dealings of a compromising nature with such a person as she considered Mr. Dalrymple to be had been the cause of this extreme reticence.

A general impression prevailed amongst the guests who had attended the ball, that the handsome ex-hussar had admired the belle of the evening to an extent that had roused the wrath of her *fiancé* against him ; but no one, strange to say, had been able to discover more than that.

Mr. Dalrymple himself never had confidantes in these matters; and Mr. Kingston, when he was enlightened at Christmas, was as little desirous as Mrs. Hardy that the facts of the case should be published. Beatrice and Rachel, who alone discussed them freely, did so with the strictest secresy.

Mrs. Reade had no confidential intercourse with her mother, as of yore, on the subject of her cousin's welfare. They had jointly resolved, just before the younger lady set out for her summer visit to Adelonga, that it would be safer to exclude Lucilla (as a married woman who told her husband everything) from any participation in the knowledge of the mischief that Mr. Dalrymple had done, and of Rachel's unfortunate infatuation for him — which did not seem so very serious at that time; and since then his name had scarcely been mentioned between them.

Now, however, the anxious little woman, with a load of care that she was by no means used to weighing on her heart, was impelled to take advantage of the opportunity offered by Lucilla's reference to that momentous ball to put a question that had suddenly become to herself, tormentingly importunate.

"Has anything been heard of that Mr. Dalrymple lately?"

"Oh, yes," said Lucilla; "he is gradually getting better."

"Getting better!" echoed Beatrice, sharply. "Why, what is the matter with him? Is he ill?"

"Didn't you hear? He had a dreadful accident. He was breaking-in a young horse that was very wild, and it bucked him off, or did something, and he fell on his head. It is a wonder he didn't break his neck.

41—2

No one saw it happen, for he was away on the plains by himself, and it was only when he did not come home at night that Mr. Gordon went to look for him. They were a long time finding him, and he had been there for hours, and he was quite insensible. There were some wild dogs sniffing at him, as if he were really dead. Indeed, Mr. Gordon said, if they hadn't found him when they did, the dingoes would probably have made an end of him. Was it not dreadful?"

Mrs. Reade was staring at the fire, not displaying that interest in the narrative that its tragic details demanded, apparently.

"When did it happen?" she asked quietly, without lifting her eyes.

" Oh, some time ago—in December. We did not hear of it until January. But he is only now able to get out of bed and crawl about, poor fellow. He was dreadfully hurt. His brain was affected, and the summer weather in that hot place was so much against him. And, of course, he couldn't have what he wanted up there, and was too bad to be moved. Mrs. Digby went there to nurse him —the Hales took the children for her. It was enough to kill her, so delicate as she is ; but she would go. She idolises him almost. Mr. Digby went with her, and stayed till the worst was over. And Mr. Gordon was most devoted — he went all the way to Melbourne to consult the doctors there about him, travelling night and day."

"Were there no doctors nearer than Melbourne?"

"Yes, of course; they had two. But he wanted the best opinions. He is Mr. Dalrymple's partner, you know, and they were old friends before they came out here."

"And did Mr. Dalrymple seem to be any better after he got the Melbourne prescriptions?"

"No; it was not a case where doctors could do much. He seemed to rally a little while Mr. Gordon was away, but he had a bad relapse afterwards. The weather became frightfully hot, and the fever of course got worse. He was delirious for a whole fortnight, and then he was so low that he just seemed sinking. However, he must be an amazingly strong

man naturally. He managed to struggle
through it, and now he is getting
about, and all danger is over, though
Mrs. Digby says he is like a walking
skeleton. I expect she will have
brought him home with her by the
time we go back; he will soon get
well when she has him in her own
house. I shall go over and see him,"
added Lucilla, compassionately; "and
I shall ask him to come to Adelonga,
as soon as he is strong enough,
and let *me* nurse him for a few
weeks."

Mrs. Reade had before her mind's
eye that photograph which her sister
had shown her in Mrs. Digby's
house. She saw every lineament of
the powerful, impressive face distinctly
—even in a photograph it was not

a face that once looked at, could be forgotten ; and she pictured to herself the changes that months of wasting illness would have made in it.

A warm rush of indignant pity, mingled with something near akin to admiration, filled her heart, which was wont to indulge itself in womanly weaknesses — an impulse to champion and befriend this man of so kingly a presence, whose sins, whatever they were, were balanced with so many misfortunes. And yet for a moment she could not help regretting that his fall from his horse had not broken his neck.

Ned, guiltily creeping into his dressing-room about half an hour later, never had the fumes of superfluous champagne dispersed from his brain so quickly. He saw his wife sitting by her own fireside, with her feet on the fender and her face in her hands, crying — actually crying — like any common woman.

# CHAPTER IV.

## "TO MEET MR. AND MRS. KINGSTON."

ACHEL was away for nearly a year and a half, seeing all the kingdoms of the earth and the glory of them in the most luxurious modern fashion. It was such a tour as a romantic and imaginative woman born to a humdrum life would feel to be the one thing to "do" and die; and according to her account, she enjoyed it extremely. She came home very

much improved by it in the opinion of
her aunt and other good judges.

"Certainly," they said, "travel is the
very best education ; there is nothing like it for enlarging the mind, and
for giving polish and repose to the
manners."

Mrs. Kingston, indeed, when she took
her place in the society of which her
husband had long been so distinguished an
ornament, was a very interesting study,
as exemplifying this soundest of popular
theories. She was greatly altered in all
sorts of ways. She had quite lost
that bashful rusticity which had been
Mrs. Hardy's despair, and in her unpretentious fashion, was really very
dignified.

There was no hurry and flutter about
her now as there used to be; none of

that indiscriminate enthusiasm, which in
her aunt's eyes branded her as a poor
relation who " had never been used to
anything nice." She expressed her appreciation of things smilingly and
sweetly, with more or less of her natural
bright frankness, but with a well-bred
moderation and serenity that might
have become a duchess. To please her
husband she wore rich raiment, "composed " by the most distinguished
Parisian artists, and it symbolised the
change that all her individuality seemed
to have undergone.

She was no longer a girl, an *ingénue*,
a bread-and-butter miss, a pretty little
nobody ; she was an experienced and
cultured woman, a leader of society,
fully equipped for that high position,
with a just appreciation of her own

importance, and relatively to that of other people's.

Indeed, there seemed to certain persons —Miss Brownlow amongst others—indications in her reticent and reposeful manner of a tendency to be exclusive, and to think a great deal too much of herself.

Mrs. Hardy, who was immensely interested in the unforeseen development, was beyond measure gratified by it— more especially as the young wife was evidently on the best of terms with her husband, though she had the good taste to refrain from drawing public attention to the fact.

Many apprehensions were set at rest by the sight of her entering a room on his arm, carefully and beautifully dressed, as if she had enjoyed dressing herself, and twinkling with diamonds everywhere, responding to respectful greetings with quiet grace, moving in her comparatively higher sphere as if she felt thoroughly at home in it. It seemed to the anxious matron that an end had been reached which justified all the means that had been taken to compass it.

Mrs. Reade was not so satisfied. She looked at the change in Rachel from another point of view. She did not like to see a girl who had been exceptionally girlish, turned into a sober woman with such unnatural rapidity.

Her sister Laura had come home, and was now settled at Kew, giving entertainments in a severely-appointed high-art house; she had had quite as much

of the education of travel as Rachel—
perhaps more, inasmuch as her young
husband was a dabbler in *bric-à-bric*,
and had a taste for old churches, and
palaces, and pictures ; whereas Mr.
Kingston's interest in foreign cities,
however famous, had chiefly concerned
itself with the quality of the society
and the cuisine of the hotels.

But Laura, though stored with information and experience, and lately
the happy mother of twin daughters,
was much the same as she had been
in her maiden days—cheerful, enter-
prising, a rider of harmless hobbies, a
great believer in herself, and in the
force and variety of her fasci-
nations.

She had improved and developed, of
course, but the experiences of travel

had not changed her as Rachel was changed.

The acute little woman who practically had never solved the meaning of love and marriage, and quite understood her disqualifications in this respect, yet had glimmerings of the state of things that existed in Rachel's heart. She knew—though she had come to the knowledge by slow degrees—that the girl was not weak all through, but only weak as the water-lily is,

" Whose root is fix'd in stable earth, whose head
Floats on the tossing waves."

And that just as she had been tenacious of certain principles in her earlier life, when living with her father in an atmosphere which she had only her own instinct to teach her was tainted with dishonour, so she would hold fast to some other things, if they had taken root, with a secret, blind integrity in spite of her emotional fluctuations in the winds and waves of circumstance.

She had adapted herself to the conditions of her marriage with the pliant submissiveness of her disposition; but there was a part of her that refused to be reconciled to all the degradation that was involved, and it was a tough and vital part of her.

Since this was violently repressed, comprehending as it did all those aspiring ideals which had had so much poetry and promise, and which represented for her, in their loss as in their possession, the meaning of human happiness and the diviner aspect of human life, there was naturally a great

vacuum somewhere—a great emptiness
for which no compensating interests were
available. Hence that serene inexpres-
siveness of mien and manner which
had so mature and distinguished an
air.

Mrs. Reade's own marriage was very
much of the same pattern in one
respect—it was but an outward and
visible sign of marriage that had no
inward and spiritual grace ; but then
she did not know what it was that she
missed, and Rachel did. And the difference between the two cases was
perfectly obvious to that intelligent
woman.

On the return of Mr. and Mrs.
Kingston to Melbourne, a number of
fashionable parties were of course given
in their honour. At the chief of these,

a great ball in the Town-hall, the dramatic action of this story, temporarily suspended by our heroine's absence from the country which held all its elements in solution, so to speak, was suddenly set going again.

It was towards the end of October, just when the gay season of the races was about to set in, and when the spring was in its glory. It strangely happened to be also the anniversary of the night of her clandestine betrothal to Roden Dalrymple, which was the memorable last time—two whole years ago—that she had seen or heard of him.

Nowadays she never mentioned Roden Dalrymple's name. She had never mentioned it to her husband since he and she came to a certain understanding on their wedding-day, and her husband had scrupulously avoided mentioning it to her; which reticence on his part was odd and uncomfortable rather than considerate and delicate, inasmuch as she was intensely anxious to pursue the line of conduct that she had laid down for herself in her relations with him—to have no secrets and to tell the truth—and to bring their companionship into such harmony and sympathy as the nature of things made possible.

And since her return she had never even suggested the existence of her lost lover to any of those who might have given her information about him —not even to Beatrice. She "would not recognise that she felt" any interest in his existence.

Nevertheless, she lived in a perpetual, absorbing, all-pervading consciousness that he and she were "in the world together," and that the key to the whole system of the universe lay somehow in that fact.

And the years and months, and days and hours were all dates in the first place, and periods of time in the second; and every date was a register of ineffaceable memories of him, which she *could* not destroy or ignore.

So on this great anniversary, as the hour approached which witnessed their last interview in the solitude of the half-built house (the boudoir was in the hands of the decorators now, and the sacred spot of floor was covered over with inlaid woodwork), she tried to put the thought of it out of her mind—tried to shut her eyes to the inevitable agonising and tantalising perception of what *might* have been—and yet was acutely responsive to every tick of the clock on her mantel-piece, checking off the reminiscent moments one by one. She followed the events of that long-ago happy night perforce as an unquiet spirit "raised" against its will.

"Now we were sitting together," she remembered, as the little clock struck nine silvery notes. "We were looking at the moonlight on the bay. Ah, me, how lovely that moonlight was !"

"Rachel," called her husband from his dressing-room within, whither he had just arrived from a dinner at the

club, "aren't you dressed yet? I met
that young woman of yours on the
stairs; she seems to have more time
on her hands than she knows
what to do with. Why don't you
make her wait on you better? She
ought to be getting you ready by this
time."

Rachel jumped up hastily and
rang for her maid, whose minis-
trations, essential to the dignity of her
present position, she certainly did not
appreciate.

"I shall not be long dressing,"
she replied; "and it is early
yet."

And then she went into his room
to ask him if he had had a pleasant
party at dinner, and whether he had
enjoyed it, anxious to show him some

special tenderness on this special night
—anxious to find some shelter in his
affection from the reminiscences that
beset her.

He was a little irritable, for his gout
was troubling him, and he did not
respond to her advances. He patted
the hand that she laid on his arm in
a perfunctory manner, and sent her
back to begin her preparations for
the ball. He did not wish her to
dress herself quickly; he wanted her
to make the most of her beauty and
her supplementary resources on such a
great occasion.

He was very fond of his wife still,
and proud of her, and good to her
in his own rather tyrannical way; but
his marriage with her, after a year
and a half of it, had become to him-

self—as under the circumstances was
inevitable — a very unromantic and
commonplace affair.

They had lived together in tolerable
peace and comfort ; they had never
quarrelled, simply because it was
Rachel's habit to efface herself at
the first symptoms of rising temper ;
but neither had they been com-
panions, in any proper sense of the
term.

As yet he had no active sense of
injury and injustice, in that the possession of his treasure gave him such
meagre compensation for all that he
had paid for it, but he did feel, in a
general way, that matrimony was—as
he confessed he had been well warned
that it would be—very tame and dull,
and uninteresting, and that it would

be too unreasonable altogether to expect a man to devote himself exclusively to its demands. Even little Rachel herself, he was quite sure, would not wish him to be bored to death.

And so he fell back insensibly into many of his old self-indulgent habits, and the pleasures of his bachelor life grew more than ever pleasant. This was particularly the case after his return to Melbourne, where his face became as familiar to club men as in the ante-nuptial days. Some excuse for this independence was supposed to lie in the fact that he and his wife had not yet settled down to housekeeping.

The Toorak mansion was being furnished and decorated with the treasures

of art and upholstery that they had
brought out with them ; and until
everything was completed, and the
entire establishment was in proper order
for their reception, and for the giving
of that magnificent house-warming to
which the world of Melbourne fashion
was looking forward, they were in-
habiting a suite of rooms in an hotel,
and domestic life, consequently, was to
a certain extent disorganised.

On this night of which we are speaking,
Rachel thought it was very kind and
attentive of him to come home to her a
full hour before he needed to have done.
It never occurred to her, any more than
to him, that he neglected her.

The servants of the hotel, who were on
the watch for a sight of her as she went
to her carriage, thought her not only one

of the most lovely, but one of the most
fortunate of women ; and so did the
majority of the gay company at the Town
Hall, when she made her appearance
amongst them.

She had come back from Europe and all
her sea-voyaging, in excellent physical
health, and the last year or two of her
life, in spite of sorrowful vicissitudes, had
ripened and developed her beauty in a
very marked degree.

She was dressed in white, but with
great richness, of course—her husband
had seen to that; covered with precious
lace, that was as attractive to the eyes of
the Melbourne ladies as the delicacy of her
pure complexion was to those of the men.
And she wore her necklace of diamond
stars, and diamonds on her arms, and on
her bosom, and in her hair ; and she was

altogether very magnificent, and made a great sensation.

Amongst her many admirers she noticed, when she had been in the room a little while, a short, stout man, of about forty or fifty years of age, apparently, who was a stranger to her, regarding her with much attention.

He had rather an air of distinction about him in spite of his low stature, and a noticeable absence of beauty; and she had a dim—very dim—impression that she had seen him, or someone like him, before.

He wore a fair moustache but no beard or whiskers, and his florid face was marked down one side with the puckered white scar of an old wound.

His eyes were quick and bright, and the keen observation that he brought to bear upon her through an eyeglass that he put into one of them whenever she came near, obviously with the intention of studying her to the best advantage, was a little disconcerting even to an acknowledged beauty.

She was waltzing with Mr. Buxton—it was her second waltz, and he danced very well—when suddenly, high in the air over her head, the great clock chimed eleven, and all the associations of that sacred hour gathered like ghosts around he rRoden Dalrymple holding the lighted match to his watch, while she sheltered the little flame from the wind—her head touching his cheek and his huge moustache as they looked down together to see the time— the mystic light and stillness of the peaceful night, through which the sound of the city bells came up to them, to warn them that their happiness was a thing too good to last.

"Eleven p.m.," he had called it; and "you must go home, little one," he had said. Could it have been at *that* moment that he meant to send her away so far, and never to take her back to his arms and his heart again?

"Aw—what's the matter? Are you dizzy?" asked her partner, feeling a break and a jar in the rhythm of the measure that had been flowing so very harmoniously.

"A little," she whispered. "I should like to sit down for a few minutes— we'll go on again, if you like, presently."

He led her to a retired bench, and while she rested stood beside her, silently watching the people who con-

tinued to revolve before them. She had
hardly sat down, and was beginning
mechanically to fan herself, when the
stranger with the eyeglass came up,
with a lady, who was also unknown to
her, on his arm.

" Here's a seat," said the little stout
man ; and his partner, an elderly and
amiable matron, sat down, bestowing
the deprecatory smile of old-fashioned
courtesy upon the two already in possession.

He took the end of the bench
himself, and chatted away to her—she
was his aunt, apparently—leaning a little
forward, with an elbow on his knee;
and Rachel, dreamily occupied as she
was, was quite conscious that his keen
eyes dwelt persistently, not upon his
neighbour's face, but upon her own.

" Why don't you go and get a partner,
James ?" said the elderly matron. " You
don't want to dance attendance upon
me, my dear—I shall do very well here
until Lucy wants me. Go and find
some pretty young lady, and enjoy yourself like the rest of them."

" I don't believe in pretty young
ladies," replied the little man, rather
bluntly. " Except Lucy—and she is
engaged for the whole night, as far as
I can make out."

Here ensued some comments upon
Lucy, who appeared to be the lady's
daughter, generally favourable to that
young person. And the little man then
began to inveigh against the abstract
girl of the period with trenchant
vigour—obviously to the great embarras-
ment of his companion, who tried her

best, but vainly, to divert him to other topics.

"In fact, there are no girls now-adays," he remarked coolly; "they are all calculating, selfish, heartless, worldly women — always excepting Lucy, of course—as soon as they cease to be children. They have only one object in life, and that is to marry a man—no, not a man necessarily, a forked stick will do—who has plenty of money."

"My dear, that is a popular senti-ment, I know, and supposed to be full of wit and wisdom, but it always seems to me that it is just a little vulgar," replied his companion, frowning sur-reptitiously, and giving uneasy sidelong glances at Rachel. "There are girls and girls, of course, just as there are men and men; we see bad and good

in every class. How beautifully this
place lights up, to be sure !"

" They like a fellow to dance with
them and dangle after them, and make
love to them, and break his heart for
them—nothing pleases them better—
when they have no serious business on
hand," the little man proceeded, with
unabashed composure, and still gazing
steadily at Rachel ; " but when it comes
to marriage—"

" My dear James, I am *not* recom-
mending marriage to you—only a
harmless waltz."

" Then they are for sale to the
highest bidder, whoever he may happen
to be. The poor, impecunious lover—
be he ever so much a lover, and
the best fellow that walks the earth
into the bargain—must take himself off

—and cut his throat for all she cares."

At this sudden change from the plural to the singular, and at something personal and impertinent that she recognised in the tone and look of the speaker, a deep blush flooded Rachel's face, and she rose from her seat with dignity, but trembling in all her limbs.

" Aw—who the dickens is that fellow?" Mr. Buxton whispered, with a scowl—supposing, however, that he could only be a disappointed aspirant for Rachel's hand. " He's an impudent brute, whoever he is, and I have a good mind to tell him so. What's his name, eh?"

" I don't know," said Rachel. But as she spoke, and was about to move away, the stranger rose and stood with an air of courteous deference to let her pass him—

an air that somehow indicated the breeding and manners of a gentleman; and all at once it flashed across her where and when she had seen him before. He was the man who had called at Toorak and been closeted with her aunt at the time when Roden Dalrymple had promised to come for her, nearly two years ago. She had gone out into the garden, thinking he might possibly have been Roden, to intercept him as he was going away. She had had only a distant glimpse of him—of his short, square figure, and the lower part of his face—but she recognised now that this was the same man. She had not gone many steps into the room, feeling strangely overwhelmed by her discovery, when a pair of exhausted waltzers went trailing by, and one of them said to the other, " Didn't somebody say Jim Gordon was

here to-night?   Where is the old fellow
hiding himself?   I should like to see him
again."

The little man with the eyeglass was—
of course he was—Roden Dalrymple's
friend and partner.

She drew her hand from her cousin's
arm, turned round, and walked deliberately back to the seat she had just
quitted.

" No," she said to her pursuing cavalier,
" do not come.   Go and dance with somebody, and fetch me presently."

" My dear Rachel, you must allow me—
aw, I couldn't really—"

"I want to speak to Mr. Gordon," she
said, pausing in front of that gentleman.
" Mr. Gordon, I want to ask you something.   Will you kindly take me out to
the lobbies—somewhere where it is quiet—

if this lady will excuse you for a few
minutes?"

Mr. Buxton was utterly bewildered, as
well he might be. He stared, stiffened
himself, and then went off to find Laura,
and to tell her of the extraordinary pro-
ceedings of her cousin "with some insolent
beggar whose name she said she didn't know,
though she addressed him by it almost in
the same breath," and to intimate (merely
by way of soothing his own injured dignity)
that there seemed to him something
" rather fishy" going on.

And Mr. Gordon, after losing his presence
of mind for about half a minute, and then
only partially recovering it, silently offered
his arm to the lady who had made that
strange appeal to him. He had never seen
her until to-night; he had hoped he never
should see her, or have anything to do with

her. She had been, in his imagination of her, the embodiment of all that was detestable in woman. But now something in the candid young face, unnaturally set and pale, and in the suppressed passion and purpose of her manner, gave him compunctious misgivings, and a vague but alarming impression that there had been some blundering somewhere.

"You are Mr. Gordon, are you not?" she began hurriedly, as soon as they were out of the crowd and glare of the ball-room. "Yes, I thought so: but I did not recognise you at first. I should have waited for an introduction, but I was afraid you might go away. I think you know who I am. What you were saying just now—had it not some reference to me?"

The little man began to stammer inco-

herently. He was completely over-
balanced by the shock of this unexpected
attack. Rachel, on the contrary, usually
so fluttered by an emergency, had a
sort of fierce, collected calm about her.

" I am sure it had," she said. " And
I want to know what you meant?"

" I—a—perhaps you are aware that
I am Mr. Dalrymple's friend, Mrs.
Kingston. I am therefore, perhaps,
something of a partisan—forgive me,
if I forgot myself for the moment—"

" Ah," she broke out sharply, " there
has been some great mistake! Tell
me—quickly—before anyone is here to
interrupt us—did you come to see my
aunt that Christmas—the Christmas
before last?"

" Certainly I came to see her and you,"
he replied.

" Did he send you ?"

" Of course he did."

" Why ?"

" Why !" he echoed angrily. " Do you mean to say you don't know why ?"

" I know *nothing*," said Rachel. She stood before him shining in her satin and diamonds, without a trace of colour in her face; and the anguish of her beseeching eyes told him plainly that she spoke the truth.

" Oh, dear me, this is terrible !" he exclaimed, in a flurry of dismay and consternation. " Do you mean to say that you didn't know that he was ill ?—that you didn't tell Mrs. Hardy to write that letter ?—that it was all done without your knowing anything about it ? Good Heavens ! would anybody believe there

were such malignant fiends in existence
—and such fools!" he added bitterly.

Then he told her the whole story—
how her lover had got hurt, and had lain
insensible for many days, between life
and death—how his first anxiety upon
recovering consciousness was about his
appointment with her—how he had de-
puted his friend to go to Melbourne and
explain his inability to keep it; and
how he (Mr. Gordon) had seen Mrs.
Hardy and afterwards Mr. Kingston, and
been led by them to an apparently un-
avoidable conclusion.

" She said you were not willing to see
me, but that she would give you my
messages and explanations," said the
little man, thinking it would be best for
his friend (and not much caring what it
would be for other people) to have it all

out at once, while he was about it ; " and that she would send me a note to the club, where I was staying, in the evening, or instruct you to do so. She had already told me that you were re-engaged to—a—your present husband. At night I got the letter, in which she repeated this assertion, stating that you had empowered her to do so."

" And you went and told him that ?"

" I did not go and tell him that—for I did not want to kill him—until I had taken every possible precaution to get it corroborated."

" Yes ?" ejaculated Rachel, breathlessly.

" I obtained an introduction to Mr. Kingston at the club, and I asked him on his honour to tell me if what Mrs. Hardy had said was true."

" You told him why you wanted to
know ?"

" I did."

She stood still for a few seconds to
collect her strength; whole years of effort
and agony were concentrated in that
little interval.

" Shall you be going back to Queensland soon ?" she asked quietly.

" I am going back to-morrow," he
said—though he had not previously
thought of doing so.

" Tell him when you see him—
tell him from me — that I never
knew *anything* — never, never, from
the day I saw him last until to-
night."

" It will break his heart to hear it,
Mrs. Kingston."

" No—he will be glad to know that

I was not utterly base. And I—I want him to know it."

"And shall I—*can* I—tell him that you were really not engaged when they said you were—when he thought you were waiting for him?"

She flushed deeply and drew herself up with a little stately gesture.

"He will not wish you to go into those particulars, Mr. Gordon. If you will give him my message simply, that is all I want you to do. He will understand it. Will you take me back to the ball-room now? I should like to find my cousin, Mrs. Reade."

# CHAPTER V.

AS nature makes us, so to a great extent, the most of us remain, when education has done its very best, or its very worst, to modify the great mother's handiwork. Her patterns, of which no one ever saw the original designs, and that have been unknown centuries a-weaving, cannot be sensibly altered in the infinitesimal fragment that one human lifetime represents, though every thread of circumstance, in its right or wrong adjustment, must have its value in the ultimate product, whatever that unimaginable thing may be.

Still, in the individual man or woman, here and there, the type that he or she belongs to is temporarily obscured by accidental causes; the lines of character, laid down by many forefathers, are twisted or straightened by violent wrenchings of irresponsible fate—as in less important branches of nature's business her processes are interrupted by lightning and earthquakes, and other rebellious forces.

Rachel, from the hour when she discovered how it was that she and Roden Dalrymple had been defrauded of their "rights," was apparently quite changed (though—as she is still a very young woman—we are not prepared to suppose that she will never be her old weak and timid and clinging self again). She was turned, from a soft and shrinking girl, into a hard and fearless, if not a defiant, woman.

The immense strength of her love—always an incalculable "unknown quantity" in the elements of human character and the factors of human destiny—had already given force and point, and meaning and dignity, to her whole personality and her relations with life; but now the magnitude of her wrongs and misfortunes, and still more of *his*, seemed to dwarf and crush every feeble trait and sentiment in her.

She went back to the ball-room, very white and silent, on Mr. Gordon's arm; and the first person of her own

party whom she met there was Mr.
Reade, under whose protection she
placed herself, dismissing her late escort
with a quiet "good-night."

She asked to be taken to Beatrice; and
Ned, who never knew from whom he had
received her, piloted her through the
crowd until he found his small wife,
whose bright eyes no sooner rested on
Rachel's face than they recognised a
new calamity.

"Has she heard anything, I
wonder?" she asked herself in
dismay. "Are you ill?" she inquired
aloud.

"I want to go home," said
Rachel.

The little woman did not waste
time asking useless questions. She
took her cousin to the cloak-room,

sent Ned for a cab, and in a few minutes the three were driving to the Kingstons' hotel.

When they reached Rachel's drawing-room, and Ned had been sent downstairs to see if her maid was on the premises, Mrs. Reade put her arms round her tenderly, and begged to know what was the matter with her.

But Rachel, singularly unresponsive to the rare caress, would not tell—would not talk at all. She would not betray the mother's crime to the daughter, and she would not mention the name of her beloved, even to her dearest friend, in these married days.

"I am not well," she said, gently but with an odd harshness in her

face and voice. "I could not dance
—I could not stay in that place. I
shall be better here. Go back, Beatrice,
and make excuses for me. Say I was
not well."

"I shall do no such thing," said
Beatrice bluntly. "I shall not leave
you until Graham comes home."

Rachel begged and protested with
a sharp peremptoriness that was very
unusual to her. Beatrice, full of
anxiety and consternation, was ob-
durate.

In the midst of their discussion,
they heard Mr. Kingston coming upstairs, bustling along in great haste.
He flung open the door, with an air
of angry irritation.

"Oh, here you are!" he exclaimed
loudly. "What on earth are you

doing? Everybody is inquiring for you, Rachel. Aren't you well? Why didn't you tell me, and let me bring you home, if you wanted to come? You have set all the room talking and gossiping, slinking off before midnight in this way—as if you were a mere nobody, who would not be missed—and not letting me know. What's the matter, eh?"

Rachel, without changing her position by a hair's breadth, lifted her eyes steadily and looked at him, but she did not speak.

Mrs. Reade saw the look, and she needed no words to tell her that some crisis in the conjugal relations of this pair had come, which no outsider had any business to see or meddle with; and she guessed correctly what it was.

"I will go back, and make what explanations are necessary," said she; "and I will come round in the morning, Rachel."

And she went out quickly, and closed the door behind her. On the stairs she met Rachel's maid going up, and told her her mistress would ring when she wanted her; and in the lobby of the hotel she replied to her husband's anxious inquiries by declaring irrelevantly that she wished Mr. Kingston, and his house and his money, were all at the bottom of the sea.

That gentleman, meanwhile, after following her out upon the landing, and looking over the stairs to see that her natural protector was in attendance, returned to his wife with a vague presentiment of unpleasantness in some shape or other.

He, too, had been struck with the peculiar expression of Rachel's face, and a guilty conscience intimated at once that she had "found out something," though it did not suggest any catastrophe in particular. There were so many things that, by unlucky accident, she might find out.

"However, I am not going to be called to account by her," he said to himself, in that spirit of swagger which she had herself nursed and nourished by her excess of wifely meekness. "*I* am not Ned Reade, to submit to be dictated to and sat upon by my own wife — so she needn't begin it."

And he walked into the drawing-room in a lordly manner.

The reception that he met with staggered him considerably.

"Graham," said Rachel, in a very quiet voice, "did you send word to Mr. Roden Dalrymple that I was engaged to you that Christmas—you know when I mean—two years ago, when I was ill? Did you tell that lie to Mr. Gordon deliberately, when you knew how things were with us?"

He was silent—intensely silent—for a few minutes, amazed, ashamed, embarrassed, and savage. He did not know how to answer her. Then he gave a little short surly laugh.

"What about it? Who has been talking to you of those things? What is Mr. Dalrymple to you *now*, I should like to know?"

" Did you ?" she persisted.

" And what if I did ?" he retorted roughly, but still making a ghastly attempt at badinage. " All's fair in love and war, you know, my dear ; and it was that aunt of yours who told the lie, as you elegantly term it—if it was a lie—not I ; I merely did not contradict her."

She looked at him steadily, with that implacable hardness in her once soft eyes.

" I will never forgive you," she said ; " I will never, never forgive you."

" I am sure I am very sorry to hear it; but I suppose I can manage to get on without your forgiveness," he began. And then he gave up trying to make a joke of it, and turned upon her savagely. " Have you been seeing that fellow, Rachel? Tell me this instant; I insist upon knowing."

"I have seen his friend," she said, quietly.

"And did he send his friend to make those explanations to you—to *you?*"

"No; he did not send him. It was by accident that I met Mr. Gordon tonight?"

"And what business had you to talk to Mr. Gordon—to talk to anybody—about your old love affairs? Do you forget that you are a married woman—that you are my wife? It was bad enough when you were single to be mixing yourself up with a disreputable scoundrel like that——"

"He is not a disreputable scoundrel,"

she interposed sternly. " He is the most
upright gentleman—he is the most noble
man—in the wide world. I might have
known," she added, drawing herself up
proudly, "that he would never have forsaken me! I might have been sure that
he would never break his word; that
whoever was to blame for what happened to me that time, *he* was not! But
I let myself be twisted round anybody's
fingers rather than trust in him. It serves
me right, it serves me right! I was not
worthy of him."

" Well—upon my word !"

" You need not look at me so, Graham.
I have never deceived *you*. I told you
before I married you exactly how it was
with me. I have never had any secrets
from you, and I never will have any. You
*know* as well as I do that I loved him—

ah! I did not love him enough, that is
what has ruined us!—and so I shall while
I live, if I live to be a hundred."

" You mean to say you can sit there and
tell me that to my face ?"

"I can only tell the truth," she replied,
with the same hard deliberation. " I
could no more help loving him, especially
now I understand how things have been
with us—no one will know it, but it will
be in my heart—than I could help
breathing. When I leave off breathing,
then I shall forget him perhaps, not
before."

Mr. Kingston was beside himself with
passion—as, indeed, so was she.

" Forewarned is forearmed," he said,
with a sort of sardonic snarl; " I shall
know now what steps to take to protect
my honour."

"You know perfectly well that your honour—what *you* call your honour—is safe," she replied proudly. "If I am not to be trusted, *he* is. Do not insult us any more. We have had enough cruelty; we shall have quite enough to bear—he and I."

And so they went on with these bitter and defiant recriminations—Mr. Kingston, of course, insisting upon giving due prominence to his own wrongs, which were very real ones in their way, and both of them making reckless proposals with respect to their domestic arrangements—until suddenly, without any apparent warning, Rachel went off into wild hysterics, and the doctor had to be sent for.

Perhaps it was the best thing that could have happened under all the circumstances. She was very ill for several hours; and in the morning, when passion was spent, and she was lying in her bed still and quiet, with her head swathed in wet bandages, her husband knelt down beside her and asked her to forgive him.

"It was for love of you that I did it," he said; "and *I* am punished, too. We can't undo it now, Rachel, if we would, and there's no good in making a public talk and scandal. Let bygones be bygones, won't you, dear?"

She lifted her heavy eyes to his face. They were cold and hard no longer, but unutterably dull and sad.

"Yes," she said wearily; "we have both been wrong; we have injured one another. We must try to make the best of it; it is the only thing we can do now."

He kissed her and stroked her face, and adjusted the wet bandages.

" There, there," he said soothingly, " we both forgot ourselves a little. We said a great deal more than we meant, I daresay. People do when they are out of temper."

And he bade her go to sleep, told her he would take her for a drive in the afternoon if she felt well enough, and went forth with the sense that he was treating her magnanimously to receive and reply to inquiries after her health in person.

By noon, " all Melbourne," according to Mrs. Hardy's calculation, was aware that Mr. and Mrs. Kingston had had a quarrel (though there was every variety of conjecture as to the cause of it, and a division of opinion as to which was the

most to blame); but it was not Mr.
Kingston's fault if all Melbourne was not
satisfied by nightfall that the quarrel had
been made up.

# CHAPTER VI.

## MRS READE MEETS HER MATCH.

"WILL Mr. Roden Dalrymple do Mrs. Edward Reade the great favour to call upon her to-morrow (Thursday) morning, if convenient to him, between ten and twelve o'clock? She is particularly anxious to see him upon a matter of private business."

This note was despatched from South Yarra to Menzies on a certain night in the early part of December, a few weeks after the Town Hall ball. Mr. Dalrymple had just come to Melbourne, and Mrs. Reade, through the gossip of afternoon visitors, had heard of it.

She had heard of a great deal more besides—from Laura's husband chiefly; and the critical nature of the situation, and her anxious solicitude for Rachel's welfare in the midst of the perils and temptations to which, while a meeting with her old lover was possible, she would be exposed, made it seem absolutely necessary that the person who was most capable of doing so effectually should interfere once more.

The course she adopted in undertaking this delicate and difficult enterprise was worthy alike of her courage and her good sense. She had never met Mr. Dalrymple, and she had no definite knowledge of his character, only an impression that he was " wild "—a man of the world, with a touch of the libertine and the vagabond about him—and that he was also undoubtedly a gentleman, with some of the finer qualities that are the heritage of good blood.

Yet she determined that she would abjure all schemes and artifices, and see him herself before there was time for anything to happen, and appeal to his honour and generosity on behalf of the woman he loved—upon whose peace it seemed evident to her he had some selfish if not distinctly evil designs.

" He has come to town in consequence of Mr. Gordon's representations, of course, for no other purpose than to see her," the little woman said to herself the moment she heard of his arrival; "and if he does see her, nothing but trouble can possibly come of it."

So she determined to prevent trouble if possible, and this seemed to her the proper way.

She prepared herself for the interview on the Thursday morning, without any sense of having undertaken a difficult task.

When he arrived she was discussing dinner with her cook, and she walked from the larder to the drawing-room with a very grave and thoughtful face, but feeling perfectly serene and self-possessed.

He was standing in the middle of the room, facing the door, with his hat in his hand when she entered. He looked immensely tall, and stiff, and stately. There was an air of impracticable independence in his attitude, and in the distant dignity of his salutation that disconcerted her a little. He was wonderfully like his photograph she thought, and yet he was a much more imposing personage than she had bargained for.

" Oh, Mr. Dalrymple—it was so kind of you to come," she said, in her quick, easy way. "I must apologise for summoning you in such a very informal manner, but—a—won't you sit down ?"

She dropped into one of her soft, low chairs ; and her visitor seated himself at a little distance from her, not hesitatingly, but with just so much deliberation as indicated a protest against the prolongation of the interview.

" I understood from your note that you

wished to see me upon some business,"
he suggested gravely.

"I did," she replied, feeling unaccountably flustered. "Perhaps you will think
it rather impertinent of me—perhaps it is
a liberty for me to take—but the fact is I
have so deep an interest in my cousin's
welfare—she is so very dear to me—I
must plead that as my excuse——"

"You are speaking of Mrs. Kingston?"
he interposed in the same cool and distant
manner, "I hope she is quite well? I
have not had the pleasure of seeing her
since her marriage."

"She is quite well, thank you. I trust
she will keep so, but I am afraid she is
not very strong. Mr. Dalrymple, I ought
perhaps to tell you that I—that Rachel
told me—that I am aware of the relation-
ship that has existed between you."

" We will not speak of that, if you please, Mrs. Reade."

" But I sent for you on purpose to speak of it."

" Then I must ask you to excuse me," he said, rising haughtily. " I cannot discuss those matters with strangers— still less with a member of Miss Fetherstonhaugh's family."

" But, Mr. Dalrymple, *I* am not to blame for anything that has happened— for any mistakes that have been made —I assure you I am not. I never knew of your accident—I never knew that Mr. Gordon came down -- I never knew anything more than Rachel did, until it was too late. And I was her intimate friend all that time, and she made me her *confidante.* I served her interests as far as a friend who loved her could, to the best of my power."

" If that is so, I am very grateful to you," he said gently, " though I am afraid you failed to see what her interests were. May I ask if you are acting under her instructions now ?  Did she authorise you to make this appointment for the purpose of speaking of these things ?"

" Of course she did not."

" Then we will not speak of them. There would be very grave impropriety in doing so.  You must see, Mrs. Reade, that nothing you can say will in the least degree affect the case for anyone.  I think we all know the truth of the story now.  It is too late to take any action one way or the other.  For Mrs. Kingston's sake, the fewer reminiscences we allow the better.  Our business is to reconcile ourselves to circumstances, since they are irrevocable, and to let the past alone. If it was your intention to explain to me that you were guiltless of active participation in the crime which parted us, believe me, I appreciate the kind motive, and I thank you from my heart. But it is much better not to say any more about it."

He was still standing with his hat in his hand, and that peculiar distant look in his sad and haughty face. Mrs. Reade sat before him in her low chair silent, with her eyes cast down.

Not one of the numerous gentlemen in whose affairs she had condescended to take an interest had ever treated her like this, and she felt inexpressibly humiliated. Yet she had no sense of resentment, strange to say, against the individual who dominated her, and the position generally, in such an unexampled manner.

" Did I understand you to say that Mrs. Kingston was not strong ?" he inquired after a short pause.

" I think she is very well," Mrs. Reade meekly responded. " Her constitution is quite sound; but her nervous system is delicate. She cannot stand worry, or shocks, or any great excitement or fatigue —any of those things upset her."

" I should imagine so. But it is always possible to keep her free of those things, is it not ?"

Mrs. Reade replied, not so much to the letter as to the spirit of the question.

" Her husband takes good care of her," she said. " He is very thoughtful for her

comfort. She does not run any risk of
harm that he can spare her. If we are
all as careful of her welfare as he is, Mr.
Dalrymple—if we are as scrupulous to
protect her peace now she is at peace——"

She broke off, and lifted her eyes wist-
fully.

Mr. Dalrymple looked down upon her
with stately and impenetrable composure.

"I am deeply thankful to know that
her marriage has so far been satisfactory,"
he said. "I suppose the house in Toorak
is nearly finished, is it not?"

"It is quite finished. They went into
it three weeks ago."

"It promised to be a very good house,
though rather of the *nouveaux riches* order
of architecture," he proceeded coolly; "and
unfortunately it is impossible to manu-

facture trees, without which the best house looks bald and naked. But it stands well. It must be a very healthy situation; and that, after all, is the principal consideration."

" I hope she will be happy in it," said Mrs. Reade. Her soul rebelled against this mode of treating the question, and yet her efforts to divert the discussion into the channels that she had designed for it were absurdly feeble and futile.

" I. hope so, indeed," he replied gravely. "I suppose you see a great deal of her, do you not?"

" Yes. I seldom miss a day without seeing her. Either I go to Toorak, or she comes here, or we meet somewhere about town. *I* do whatever is in my power to help to make her happy."

"It must be a happiness to you, too,
to have her friendship and confidence in
such a marked degree."

"It is," said Mrs. Reade.

"I—if you will excuse me—I will say
good morning. Allow me to thank you
very much for permitting me to call,
and for your kind interest in my misfortunes—and in Mrs. Kingston's welfare.
But the greatest service you can do
her, Mrs. Reade, is to be silent yourself, and to discourage gossip in others,
about anything that occurred either
before or since her marriage in con-
nection with me. I hope I do not seem
discourteous in saying this—if so, pray
forgive me. I speak to you frankly,
because you are her friend. I am
afraid she has not had many friends—
there is the more reason that we who

desire her welfare and happiness, should take every precaution against imperilling it by allowing any hint of these private matters to reach the ears of vulgar scandalmongers. A great crime has been done, for which if there is anything in the theory of retribution, some one will have to answer some day; but in the meantime our part is to take care that *she* is spared as much difficulty and suffering as possible."

"Yes, Mr. Dalrymple. That is what I think—that is what I was going to say."

"I am sure you think so. I am sure you see that that is all we can do for her now. Good morning. I am much obliged to you for your kindness. It looks rather as if we were going to have a storm, does it not? The air is close and sultry, and the glass is falling very fast."

He turned from looking out of the window and made a stately bow; she laid her hand upon the bell mechanically —she had no arts wherewith to keep him; and in another minute he had passed out of the house, and the door was shut upon him. The interview which was to have had such great results was over.

We have heard it said of a pioneer colonist, lessee of a Crown-land principality, that, after bearing the reverses of fortune which, with the advent of free selectors, overwhelmed him, the loss of land and stock and the accumulated treasure of toilsome and prosperous years, with the fortitude and equanimity of a gentleman, he was broken down at last by the unspeakable humiliation of the circumstance that he had " lived to hear himself called a boss-cocky."

Mrs. Reade had not only been defied and defeated, and made to feel small and ridiculous in her own drawing-room, where never man or woman—man, especially— had never dared dispute her supremacy ; but she had lived to hear herself called, or at any rate to find herself considered, a *gossip*—a common tattler and busybody, who intrigued in other people's private affairs from the vulgar feminine love of meddling—and the blow was equally bitter.

She stood in the bow window of her drawing-room, and watched the tall figure leisurely striding through the garden as if South Yarra and the adjacent suburbs

were but a small part of his possessions;
taking in all the details of his strong majestic figure, his thin, dark, proud face,
with its immense moustache, the perfection of his quiet dress, and the repose
and dignity of his bearing generally,
and of every distinct movement that he
made—even when trying to open a
gate with a mysterious fastening, at
which most people fumbled and bungled
awkwardly.

But she was *not* consumed with a
passion of angry resentment against him
for the indignities and humiliations that
he had heaped upon her. No, she was
filled with a vague but intense respect
and admiration for him, a feeling that
she had never before entertained for any
individual of his sex.

She did not say it to herself in so many

words, but the thought of her heart undoubtedly was that here was the man,
who as a husband, would just have suited
her.

## CHAPTER VII.

### GOOD-BYE.

N that same day, at a little after four o'clock in the afternoon, Mrs. Kingston might have been seen—she *was* seen, in fact—going into the Town Hall by herself, having left her carriage in the street below. She mounted the stone steps lightly, with the train of her dress held up in her hand, looking exquisitely fresh and dainty in the dusty sultriness that everywhere prevailed; and she glided through the vestibule as if time

46—2

were precious, paid her sixpence, and entered the hall, where she took a solitary seat under the shadow of the gallery at the lower end.

The organist was interpreting Mozart to some hundreds of receptive citizens, making the great organ sing like a choir of angels in the " Gloria " of the Twelfth Mass, "*et in terra pax, pax, pax hominibus; bonæ, bonæ voluntatis.*" All the spacious place was flooded with the impassioned harmonies of that inspired theme.

Rachel was not what is popularly called musical, but in the dulness of her empty life her soul slacked its thirst in this way, as a soul of a lower order, which had been denied its natural nourishment, might have found comfort in the emotional stimulus of champagne or brandy.

She could not play well herself, but she was like a fine instrument to be played upon; not one sweet phrase of melody passed from her listening ear to her sensitive heart without wakening an echo that had the very divine afflatus in it in response. And in this resonance of enthusiasms and aspirations, dumb and suffocated in the bondage of her artificial life—in the sense of breathing spiritual air, and freedom, though with a passion of enjoyment that filled her with far more pain than peace—she found the one true luxury of her much-envied lot.

Long ago—oh, so long ago !—the music of a violin had led her into enchantment, as the Pied Piper of Hamelin led away the children. To-day the music of the Town Hall organ, speaking now in Mozart's dramatic choruses, and again in Baptiste's Andante in G, was a similar but a sadder incantation.

She sat solitary in her far-away chair, with her feet on the rung of the one in front of her, her hands, gloved to perfection, folded in her lap, her delicate, neat dress daintily adjusted, much as she might have sat in the pew at church, a model of matronly grace and propriety.

But who could tell, from the expression of her quiet *pose* and her dreamy eyes, what ineffable raptures and fancies, what infinite longings and yearnings—nameless, even to her own consciousness, but all reminiscent of the blessed past—soared out of captivity on the wings of those alluring harmonies !

Who could see that in her heart she

was crying — crying bitterly — for the poetry and the beauty that were lost out of her life !

There was an interval of silence, during which she sat quite still, looking at the great organ-pipes, and seeing nothing; and then there grew out of the hush the delicious rhythm of the " Faust " waltz, beating like a soft pulse through the summer air.

What spell is there in the " Faust " waltz, or in any waltz, for one whose heart is capable of receiving and responding to the inspired message of Mozart?

How can we tell ? But this we know, that those whose hearts are warm and young—who understand how to love and how to dance, and have done the two things at the self-same moment—have seldom any more power than they have

honest inclination to resist the subtle wiles
of this simple measure.

There is a vox humana stop out in
whatever organ plays it, magnetic to the
human passions that memory and imagination keep. Rachel did not ask why it
was, but she felt, as soon as the air began
to unwind itself from a confusion of sweet
sounds, and she heard the slow time
throbbing softly in her ears, that she did
not know how to bear it.

It filled her soul with a great wave of
suffocating emotion—it ran like an electric
current over all her sensitive nerves—it
contracted her white throat with a choking
pain that was like incipient hysteria—it
set abnormal pulses bounding in her brain.
She did not think of Adelonga, and the
hour when she and her true love had their
first and last waltz together.

No definite picture of the past arose at
the magician's bidding, or if it did, she
shut her eyes to it. But she could not
help the forlorn rapture of longing for
that nameless something that was the
most precious of her woman's rights,
which fate and fraud had taken from
her, when the notes of this dreamy waltz
measure, so charged with passionate and
poetic associations, pulsed from the
heart of the organ into her warm young
blood.

"Oh, my love! my love!"—that was
the burden of the music which was not
set to words.

And she turned her face a little, and
saw Roden Dalrymple standing in the
doorway. He had come in quietly, and
was waiting, with his hat in his hand,
apparently for a pause in the performance,

which he did not wish to interrupt, but
really until he could find where some
one whom he was looking for was
sitting.

It was the first time she had seen him
since that October night when they had
parted in the moonlight under the walls
of the house that was now her home ; but
she had been, unknown to herself, expect-
ing him, and there was no shock in her
surprise.

She knew that he was looking for her,
when she saw his eyes travelling over the
rows of occupied chairs in the upper
division of the hall, and she longed to call
out to him,

"Roden, Roden, here I am !"

But not a dozen seconds passed before
he saw her far away from him in her
shadowy corner ; and when he saw her,

with that solemn eagerness in her face, he knew—but he said to himself he had already known—that, though she had forsaken him, she had never done him wrong.

Of course before the day was over it was reported in various circles, more or less select, that pretty Mrs. Kingston, who had married an old fogey for his money, was in the habit of coming to the organ recitals alone and unbeknown to her husband, in order to enjoy clandestine flirtations with younger and more fascinating men.

It was also darkly whispered that the favoured individual was a person who made it his constant practice to run away with married women, and to murder their lawful spouses in sham duels afterwards if they ventured to make any objections.

But of all the human beings collected in the Town Hall that afternoon, perhaps no two were less capable of violating the spirit of the moral and social law whereof the letter is so sacred to the ubiquitous and lynx-eyed Mrs. Grundy, who persists in suspecting everyone of a desire to evade or infringe it, simply for the sake of doing so, whenever he or she is presented with an opportunity.

That they loved one another as much as it was possible for sympathetic hearts to love, and that they seized one brief half-hour out of a lifetime of separation in which to say farewell, might have been reprehensible from the conventional point of view; but then the conventional point of view does not embrace the universe, by a very long way.

He came down the hall, and round to her chair, and she drew her dress close that he might sit down beside her. She was too innately pure to make any mere outward and artificial demonstrations of modesty in such a moment as this; and she trusted him too well to be afraid of him.

She put out her hand, and he took it in a long, close clasp; and they looked at one another the while with loving, despairing eyes, which said, " Oh, Rachel, why *did* you?" and " Oh, Roden, forgive me !" and bridged the only gulf that could be bridged between them, without any help of words.

And then, though the organ began to

fill the air with the soronous crash and
thunder of Bach's great pedal fugue in
D, they heard nothing but the beating
of their hearts, and the memories that
called to them from their brief past,
vibrating through the void and silence
of a world in which they were alone
together.

When the music ceased for an interval,
Mr. Dalrymple rested his arm on the
back of the chair which had served
Rachel for a footstool, and looking into
her face, said under his breath,

"Gordon gave me your message—I
came down to thank you — and I
thought we should get on better if
we could see each other just once.
Dear, we must try and comfort ourselves with knowing that neither of us
played the other false."

"*I* did — *I* did," she whispered
hurriedly. "1 ought to have trusted
you, Roden."

"Yes—that was a mistake. But you
did not know any better, poor child.
And they were too many for you,
those people. Gordon ought to have
insisted on seeing you, himself, or
getting some message to you, and not
have left you in their hands. But he
did his best, he says. He was too
anxious to get back to me to have
much patience over it, and he didn't
bargain for being told lies of that
magnitude in cold blood. However,—
however——"

He broke off and looked at her with
a passion of love and grief in his eyes
that he dared not trust to speech. And
she looked back at him, with her

simple soul laid bare—longing to make
him know, if they were never to be
together like this again, how absolutely
in her heart she had been true to him.
*She* would not tell him a lie, at any rate.

" Oh," he said in a sort of groaning
whisper, drawing a long hard breath,
" oh, my little one, isn't it hard
lines !"

" Don't," she gasped, feeling that
clutch on her throat tighten with a
sudden spasm ; " oh, Roden, don't !"

And he straightened himself quickly,
and sat back in his chair. And the
organ began to play again—a stately
march of Schubert's, which acted like
a tonic on her disordered nerves, and
as a sedative to the hysterical excitement
that for a moment had threatened to
overmaster her.

The echoes of that march rang in her ears, when Roden was gone back to Queensland and this chapter of her life was finished, for many a long day.

And then at last the thunders of the National Anthem brought the performance to a close, and the audience trooped out, casting curious glances as they went at the distinguished-looking couple standing conspicuously apart— the tall stranger with the peculiar moustache, who had soldier and gentleman written on him from head to foot, and the graceful young lady with the lovely complexion and the irreproachable French dress, whom nobody "who was anybody" failed to recognise.

The two were left together amongst all the empty chairs, in a silence that

was hardly broken by the organist's
movements at the far end of the hall,
closing the stops and keys of his
enormous instrument.

"Well," said Mr. Dalrymple, looking
down upon his companion, who lifted
to his sombre eyes a pale but
solemn face, "well—so this is all, I
suppose!"

Her lips twitched a little; she could
not answer him.

"You are not sorry that I came, are
you, Rachel? It will not make it harder
for you, will it?"

"Oh, *no*, Roden! But it is *you* on
whom it is so hard—you will be so
lonely without me! I can't bear to
think what I have brought on you
—and you had so many troubles
already!"

"Not you, dear—not you. And I can bear all my part of it, if only things go well with you."

"Why did you break that trace?" she exclaimed, with a touch of bitter passion. "But for that—but for two minutes lost—you would never have seen me, and then I should never have spoiled your life like this."

"But, dear, we are not going to regret *that*, I hope. We have got something 'saved from chance and change,' if not much, that to me at any rate—yes and to you too, I know—is worth even this heavy price that we are paying for it now. It need not spoil our lives, Rachel, to know—what we know. It is an agonising thing to see how blessed it *might* have been for us, and to be obliged to give it all up; but I shall

47—2

never think of those two hours, when
we belonged entirely to each other—only
two hours, Rachel, out of our whole
lives!—without being thankful for the
chance which gave them to us. Yes, and
I think we shall be the better for them
—I don't say happier, because I really
don't know what that word means—
but I think life will somehow have
a finer quality henceforth, whatever
happens, on account of those two hours.
Dear, I am forcing myself to give in
to the hard fate that has done us out
of our inheritance; but there is one
thing that I don't think I *could* get
reconciled to—and that is to thinking
that you would ever live to wish
that we had never known each
other."

"I could not wish it," she whispered;

" I could only try to persuade myself that I did."

" Do not try. You are under no obligation of duty to do that. Try to be happy with your husband—try not to fret over what is irrevocable, and not to hanker after what is hopeless. But don't try to turn me out of the only place in your life where I have a corner of my own. Let me keep the little of you that I have got—it is little enough! Do you remember what you said to me that night ?—you said you had no rights in my past. *He* has no rights in our past. Keep it sacred, Rachel, for my sake. That will not hurt anybody. You are not afraid that such remembrances, if you shut them away in your heart, will militate against your efforts to do what is right by him ? And you are not afraid that *I* will ever tempt or trouble you ?"

" Oh, Roden, I am not afraid of you— you well know that!"

" Treat me as if I were dead," he said gently. " If I had been killed that time when I was thrown—if I were in my grave now—I know how you would think of me. You would not wish you had never seen me then. That is how I *want* you to think of me, Rachel."

" I know," she said, drawing a deep breath. " But to me—even if you *had* killed yourself—to me you could never be dead."

By this time they had sauntered slowly out of the deserted hall and through the empty vestibules, and were standing in the doorway, looking out upon the street below them.

The storm that had threatened in the morning was gathering up. Heavy clouds weighed upon the sultry air, and gusts of wind were beginning to blow the dust about ominously. Pedestrians were hurrying to gain shelter before the rain came on, but, as they passed, they took note of the lingering pair, who were apparently heedless of the warnings of the elements, with more or less curious eyes. Neither of them, it is needless to say, minded in the least who saw them. They had no desire to take even this last good-bye clandestinely.

And when Rachel, to whom it had not occurred to wonder why her carriage was not in attendance, saw it thundering along the street towards her, it was with as much relief as surprise that she recognised her husband in it, looking out of the window for her.

"We have said nothing," said Mr. Dalrymple, who perceived the approach of his old rival and enemy; "and we had so much to say."

"Perhaps it is better not to say much," said Rachel.

"Perhaps so. But one thing you must not mind my asking you—and I know you will tell me truly—are you getting along pretty well? Do you think you will be able to make anything of a happy life out of it? That is my great anxiety."

"Do not be anxious about me," she replied. "I shall get along. I know that you forgive me—that will help me more than anything."

"Don't talk about forgiveness, child—

it implies a wider separation than I think has ever been between us. There can be no forgiveness in the case of people who never knowingly do one another wrong."

The carriage, with its high stepping, showy horses, began to slacken speed, and they descended the long flight of steps quietly, side by side.

"Is he good to you?" inquired Roden, quickly.

"Very," she replied; "very, indeed."

And then they reached the pavement, and the person referred to got out of the carriage and came to meet them.

It must be recorded, to Mr. Kingston's credit, that he behaved like a gentleman on this occasion. He was a little acid and supercilious, and not as composed as he assumed to be; but otherwise he conducted himself with propriety. " I took the carriage for half an hour," said he loudly. " I hope I haven't kept you waiting, my dear. Ah, Mr. Dalrymple, how do you do? I did not know you were in town. I hope you are quite well. Making a long stay?"

" A day or two only," said Roden, who stiffened in spite of himself, but spoke with studied courtesy. " I shall be starting back to Queensland to-night. I am glad to have had the opportunity of meeting Mrs. Kingston, and to see her looking well."

" Oh, yes, she is very well, I hope. Travelling did her good—it does everybody good. I felt quite set up by it myself. Dear me, was that a drop of rain? I think you had better be getting home, Rachel. There is a heavy storm coming directly. Good day, Mr. Dalrymple, good day. We can't set you down anywhere, I suppose?"

Mr. Dalrymple declined a seat in the carriage with thanks, and he held out his hand to Rachel.

"Good-bye," he said quietly.

"Good-bye," she replied, with an ash-white face. They looked at one another for a second; and then, lifting his hat gravely, Mr. Dalrymple turned and walked away down the street, and Mr. Kingston gave his arm to his wife, and led her to her carriage. Poor Rachel! she did not ask herself what would happen next—she did not wonder nor care whether she was to be scolded or not. For a few bitter, lonely moments, she had no recognisable future.

Then she turned to her husband, who was fanning the fuel of his wrath in silence, laid her hand on his arm, and said softly, "Graham?"

"Well—what?" he inquired, roughly.

"Do not be angry. I am never going to see him again."

"It's to be hoped not," he snarled, "if you have any regard for your reputation. Standing up there with him, in that public way, for all Melbourne to see!"

"You would not have wished me to meet Mr. Dalrymple in any way that was *not* public," she said, drawing herself up. "And I should be very sorry to do anything that all Melbourne might not see."

The rain began to sweep down heavily, and he turned to put up the window nearest him with an energy that threatened destruction to the glass.

And he said no more about Mr. Dalrymple.

Disturbed as he was, he was greatly relieved that the meeting he had always dreaded was over, and had taken place so quietly; and poor as was his estimation of the abstract woman, he had the most implicit faith in his wife's sincerity.

When she told him that she had bidden her old lover a final farewell, he believed her; and, though the sight and thought of the man made him ferocious, he was quite aware that difficulties were adjusting themselves more satisfactorily than he could have expected.

He did not feel that he had any excuse for upbraiding Rachel now, and he did not do it. But he had to put great restraint upon himself not to do it.

He got out of the carriage at his club, shutting the door with a bang behind him, and while his wife drove home by herself in a state of semi-consciousness, he went in to quarrel with some of his old friends who chanced to require his opinion upon the political situation. Politics, he promptly gave them to understand, were beneath his notice, likewise the people who concerned themselves therein. He wouldn't touch one of them with a pair of tongs. It wasn't for gentlemen and clubmen to mix themselves up with a lot of rogues and vagabonds. Let them alone and be

hanged to them. That was what
respectable people did in America. If
Americans didn't care what riff-raff
represented them, why should they?

As for the colony, if it liked to be
dragged in the dirt—if it preferred, of
its own free will, to go to the devil—
let it, for all to him.

And so he worked off his savage temper
harmlessly, and appeared in his own
drawing-room at seven o'clock, irreproach-
ably spruce, and with a flower in his
button-hole, looking jaunty and amiable,
as if nothing had happened.

Rachel, when he arrived, was sitting
alone in the midst of her wealth and
splendour, waiting for him.

She rose as he entered and went to
meet him, looking lovely in her favourite
black velvet, with red geraniums in her

hair; and she laid her hand on his sleeve, and lifted a sad but peaceful face. "Kiss me, Graham," she said gently.

He put his arms round her at once.

"Dear little woman!" he responded. "I understand. I am not angry with you. It's all right. We won't say any more about it."

And he led her to the dining-room and placed her "at the head of the table," which was her social throne; and he plied her with dainty viands and rare wines with a fussy solicitude that was highly edifying to the servants who waited upon them, by way of showing her that he forgave her.

He was much impressed by his own large magnanimity; and what was more

to the purpose, so in her unselfish heart,
was she. They spent the evening together,
*tête-à-tête* by the fireside (for it was cold
when the storm was over), in the most
domestic manner, planning new schemes
for the garden and for the arrangement
of a pet cabinet of blue china; and
when Rachel went to bed, lighting her
way about the great corridors and stair-
cases with a candle that her husband
had lit for her, she felt that he was
helping her to make a fair start upon
the weary road which stretched, plain
and straight—but, oh, so flat and bare!—
before her.

And she was very grateful to him.

Mr. Dalrymple, meanwhile left town by
an evening train, and travelled night and
day until he reached his home in the
Queensland wilderness, where, being

human—and very much so, too—he un-
loosed his heart from the restraints that
he had put upon it, and railed at ease over
the injustices of fate in the very strongest
language.

" Why should I have done it?" he demanded of his ancient friend and comrade
as they lounged in restful attitudes under
the grass-thatched verandah of their
humble little house, smoking the pipe of
peace in the cool of the summer day.
" Why should I have given her up to him?
What right has he to keep her, while I am
lonely for the rest of my days? He has not
the shadow of a right. She doesn't belong
to him, and she never will. There is no
binding force in any other contract that is
entered into by fraud and false pretences;
why should there be in this which she
has been dragged into, and which deprives

her as well as me, of all the flower and sweetness of her life? It is a monstrous sacrifice—and as immoral as it is monstrous.

"It isn't as if we had no end of years, no end of lives to throw away. Suppose, ages hence, if we should survive, with our human nature, and I, for one, don't want to survive without it—and we look back upon this precious bit of certain happiness that we *might* have had, and see that we voluntarily gave up the whole of it merely because of a wretched little paper law—a miserable little conventional prejudice—what shall we think of ourselves then? We shall say that we did not deserve a gift that we did not know how to value."

"Rave away," said Mr. Gordon. "It will do you good. All the same, you

know, as well as I do, that it would be
impossible for you to do less or more than
you have done."

Of course it was impossible. Few
people are better than they profess to be,
but he was one of those few. And if he
had had the happiness of twenty lives to
lose, he would have lost it all twice over
rather than have kept it at any cost of
peace or honour to the woman he loved.
He allowed himself the right to love her
still, which, as he justly remarked, couldn't
hurt anybody.

He thought of her as he rode about his
lonely plains, looking after black boys and
cattle, and dreamt of her as he lay out in
the starlight nights, with a saddle for his
pillow, and the red light of the camp-fire
flickering through the darkness upon his
face ; and always with a sense that,

spiritually and morally, she belonged, before all the world to him.

But he never at heart regretted either that he had seen her that day at the Town-hall, or that he had elected to see her no more. He had done the only thing that it had been in him to do.

# CHAPTER VIII.

### CONSOLATION.

IF it is true, as it is said, and as the observation of most of us seems to testify, that the ideal marriage is hardly ever realised, and then only when the rare and brief experience has been bought at untold cost of precious years, it is, perhaps, equally true that the majority of marriages wrongly and recklessly entered into, provided the contracting parties are honestly disposed, turn out surprisingly and undeservedly well.

Time, which solaces our disappointments and sanctifies our bereavements, remedies also in a great measure even these criminal mistakes.

As Rachel truly said, there are " whole worlds of things " besides love —*i.e.,* " the love of man and woman when they love their best "—to knit husbands and wives together ; and, independently of the ties that children create, and which, to the mother at least, are supremely and eternally sacred, the innumerable soft webs of habit and association that are woven in days and years of intimate companionship grow, like ivy over a fissure in a wall, so strong as eventually not only to hide the vacant place, but in some degree to supply artificially that element of stability and permanence to the structure which in its essential substance it lacked.

And so it was with Rachel. After a little time, when she had "settled down," changed and aged, and sobered as she was, she really was not unhappy.

She was always vastly conscious of her loss, but she was of two wholesome a disposition to be embittered by it; and her simple sense of duty and her characteristic unselfishness prompted her from the first to wear a cheerful face for her husband, and never by word or deed to reproach him, which course of conduct had the natural result of comforting herself quite as much as it gratified him.

He was not a bad man, and in his easy fashion, he loved her.; and appreciating her gentle and dutiful behaviour, he put himself out of the way to be kind to her, though, with all his attentions, he never was what one would call a domestic husband.

Her demands upon him were not exorbitant. Indeed, she was true to her creed in not demanding anything; but for such evidences of his affection as he voluntarily bestowed upon her she showed herself always grateful

in a meek, pleased way that was very
charming to a man vain of his own
importance, and she did not profess
to be more so than, in her soft heart,
she really was.

She had no vocation for independence,
nor for making herself—still less for
making others—miserable ; and if she
had married Bluebeard instead of a
well-intentioned gentleman, she must
have twined herself about him with
her tender, deferential, delicately-
caressing ways—which came as naturally to her as breathing — and have
found support and rest in doing
it.

When all signs of storm had cleared
away, the apparently ill-matched husband and wife settled down to a life

together that, if not rapturously delightful, was quite as placid and kindly and
peaceful as the married life of most
of us.

They did not see a great deal of
each other, to be sure; but the hours
that they spent together, being generally
hours when Mr. Kingston was tired
or unwell, and wanted to be nursed
and cheered, and to have the papers
read to him, had a homely sweetness
and solace for Rachel not far removed
from happiness.

And then I am afraid it must be
confessed that the house, and the
wealth and luxury belonging to it, *did*
comfort her a little.

She was excessively unpretentious in
her habits, and pure and simple in her

tastes, but she had an intense appreciation of all those delicate personal
refinements which womanly women
love, and only those who have money,
and plenty of it, can enjoy—of which
years of sordid poverty had taught her
the grace and value; and it was not
possible to her, with her healthy sense
of life, to refuse, even if she had
wished, to absorb the fragrance and
brightness of her social and material
surroundings.

She revelled in her beautiful garden
and in her spacious and artistic rooms;
she loved her piano and her books
and pictures, and her innumerable
pretty things; she enjoyed her drives
and her rides, and her visiting and
her parties, and her operas and con-
certs, and her shopping expeditions—

upon which no limitations were placed
by her husband, who liked her
to spend his money—with Laura and
Beatrice.

And, more than all, she delighted
in the power which her position gave
her of doing all kinds of helpful,
unpretentious service to the poor and
miserable, whom she seemed, by a sort
of divining-rod, to discover in the most
unexpected places.

Her husband would not allow her
to make her large subscriptions to the
public charities anonymously, nor would
he consent to her taking invalids of
the lower orders for drives, except
upon unfrequented roads and in a
generally surreptitious manner; and he
strongly objected to her visiting poor

people's cottages, and running risks of catching dirt and fever.

But she might make frocks for ragged children, and babyclothes for unprovided mothers, and scrap-books for the Alfred Hospital ; she might load her carriage with wine and chicken broth every time she went out; she might spend a little fortune, as she did, in helping on benevolent enterprises of all sorts; and he only laughed at her for being a soft-hearted little goose, and triumphed over her when —as happened in five cases out of ten—she was proved to have been more or less flagrantly imposed upon and taken in.

Like most people who have badly known the want of money, she was decidedly extravagant in spending it now that she had plenty; and, unlike most husbands and wives in such circumstances, she and Mr. Kingston had no pleasanter episodes in their domestic life than those which had reference to her financial embarrassments.

It was charming to him (since his banking account was much too solid to be easily affected by her operations) to see her come, with her timid and anxious face, to confess that she had spent all her money, and to ask him, with the sweetest wifely meekness, if he could spare her a little more; and to her he never showed to better advantage than when he declared, so obviously without meaning it, that she would ruin him, and then gave her twice as much as she had asked for.

She always flushed and glowed with pleasure at this delicate and generous, and gentlemanly way of doing things, and would put her arms round his neck and kiss him; and, naturally, he would thereafter set forth to his club, feeling proud of himself and pleased with things in general, his young wife and he being so thoroughly in their right places in their relation to one another.

And then there came to Rachel that which to every true woman is the greatest and dearest and best—save one—of all life's many good things, and which to her must inevitably have made even the most loveless marriage lovely :—

" On the 17th inst., at Toorak, the wife of Graham Kingston, Esq., of a son."

This little notice appeared in " The Argus," of the 18th, and caused a flutter and sensation in all well-regulated Melbourne households.

" Dear me, how nice! and a son, too. How pleased Mr. Kingston will be! An heir to all that fine property at last! Dear me, how nice! We must call and make inquiries."

And when kind inquiries resulted in the satisfactory information that both mother and infant were progressing favourably, society congratulated Mr. Kingston with effusive and impressive cordiality, which that gentleman, deprecating a fuss with airs of smiling indifference, felt to be by no means more than the occasion demanded.

Of course, the interesting event made a pleasant commotion in the great Toorak house and in the Hardy family.

Mrs. Hardy assumed the functions of mother-in-law to Mr. Kingston, and introduced him to his son and heir with a genuine maternal pride, that could not have been more touching or more complimentary to either of the delighted parents, had the featureless little atom been a lineal fifth grandchild.

The stately matron, as is the habit of stately matrons under such circum-

stances, put off her conventional armour
and rustled softly about the hushed
rooms, clothed in all the homely woman-
liness of her own baby-nursing youth;
and Rachel, watching her from her
tranquil nest of pillows, forgave her—
as she had long ago forgiven her
husband—and wondered that she had
never understood before what a truly
sweet and loveable woman dear Aunt
Elizabeth was.

And Laura came up to see the
baby, bringing a wonderful high-art
coverlid for the cradle, and all sorts
of wise advice (based upon her ex-
ceptional experience as the mother of
twins).

And Beatrice came—poor Beatrice,
who had no babies!—and held the tiny

creature for a long time in her arms, looking with silent wistfulness at its crumpled little face.

And by and bye, when Rachel was promoted to gorgeous dressing-gowns and a sofa in her boudoir, Lucilla came to stay with her, full of importance and responsibility (as the mother of the largest family of them all), to instruct her in the newest and most improved principles upon which an infant of quality should be reared.

As if Rachel wanted showing how to manage a baby ! Some ladies, as the nurse sagely remarked, never had any sense, but if Mrs. Kingston had been a poor man's wife, which she hoped she would excuse her taking the liberty of speaking of such a thing, she couldn't have took to the child more naturally.

It speedily became apparent to others besides that experienced woman that maternity was Rachel's vocation, and, when she found it, it seemed that she had found a consolation, if not an actual compensation, at last for the great want and sorrow of her woman's life.

Mrs. Hardy, watching the young mother's passion of tender solicitude for the baby that she could hardly bear to have five minutes out of her sight, told herself that, after all, the end *had* justified the means; and even Mrs. Reade, who was most interested in this latest experiment of a benevolent Fate,

came practically to the same conclusion.

One day she was alone with her
cousin. Rachel had been entertaining
a small and select circle at afternoon
tea in her own pretty room, and the
baby had been present, and she had
been pointing out to its father what
lovely eyes it had, and what small
ears, and what perfectly-shaped hands,
and how charming it was altogether—
much to Mr. Kingston's amusement, and
obviously to his immense satisfaction also ;
and now he had kissed her affectionately
and gone out, and the baby was taking
a siesta, and she was resting on her
sofa by the fireside, gazing at the bright
logs meditatively, with a half smile on her
face.

"Tell me," said Beatrice, suddenly, crossing the hearth and kneeling down beside her; "tell me, are you happy now, Rachel?"

Rachel lifted her soft eyes, shining with a sort of vague rapture.

"Oh, yes," she said, quickly; "indeed I am." And then in a moment her face was overshadowed, and she looked in the fire again with eyes that shone with tears. "I am *too* happy," she said, under her breath, "while he is alone and sad."

"Don't you think he will like you to be as happy as possible?"

"I know he will. But it lies on my heart that he is desolate while I have so many consolations. Beatrice, I was reading some verses of Emily Brontë's

the other day, and they seemed to express
exactly how it is with me. Do you remember them?

" ' Sweet love of youth, forgive, if I forget thee,
      While the world's tide is bearing me along;
   Other desires and other hopes beset me,
      Hopes that obscure, but cannot do thee wrong.'

Oh my love!" she broke out suddenly,
"I do not forget thee! And," she
added, more quietly, "1 don't think
my being happy can wrong him,
Beatrice."

"No, dear child, far from it," said
Mrs. Reade.

The little woman was not shocked,
nor was she dissatisfied with the
state of things that this naïve re-
velation disclosed to her. She was

deeply thankful to know that Rachel, after all, was happy; but she was not sorry to know also that she was to this extent faithful to her true love, who had dealt so well by her.

It was at this very hour that the papers containing the announcement of the baby's birth arrived at the Queensland bungalow, and that Roden Dalrymple learned what a change had taken place, not only in the life and welfare of his beloved, but in his own lonely and empty lot.

"The wife of Graham Kingston, of a son." He knew as well as anybody—better even than Rachel herself—what that little notice meant. It meant that the gulf already parting them had all at once widened to an immeasurable extent.

He knew how it would be with that
tender and clinging heart—it would be
able to solace itself now, even for the
loss of him.

Yet he loved her well enough to be
glad and thankful for the comfort that
had come to her, though the coming of
it left him doubly bereaved.

# CHAPTER IX.

## REPARATION.

BUT, after all, Fate willed that this marriage should be but the chief episode in the story, and not the story itself, of Rachel's life.

One day, when she was flitting about her great drawing-room, with a basket of flowers on her arm, singing soft airs from "Don Giovanni" under her breath as she busied herself with the arrangement of little groups of leaves and flowers in sundry precious receptacles here and there, a footman entered with a telegram.

"That is from your master," said Rachel, lifting it from the salver and tearing off the envelope.

"Wait a moment, James, until I see if there are any orders for you to take out."

She put down her flowers on the piano, read the brief message tranquilly, and then lifted her face with a smile.

"Ask Wilkinson to have the carriage ready at three o'clock," she said; "not the brougham, if it keeps as fine as it is now, the open carriage. And tell cook I want to speak to her in half an hour.

Your master is coming home to-day instead of Friday."

James said "Yes'm" and retired, and his mistress continued her occupation of arranging the flowers with more haste and eagerness than before.

Mr. Kingston had gone from home a few days previously to meet some distinguished foreign visitors at a friend's house in the country, a thing he did not often do, and she had stayed behind because little Alfred seemed to have symptoms of a bad cold coming on—which, however, had been happily checked at that stage.

She had not expected her lord's return just yet, but she concluded that he had not found the party amusing, or had been bored in some way, and so had excused himself from prolonging his visit; and she was glad of the accident, whatever it was, that was bringing him back so soon.

In the afternoon she went upstairs to get ready to go to the station to meet him. It was winter, and she clothed herself in rich furs—sealskin and sable, with the sealskin cap of old days on her shining head—against which the soft roundness of her cheek and throat, and the blush-rose delicacy of her complexion was particularly distinct and striking, and also the evident fact that, far from pining away, she had developed in health and strength quite as much as in beauty during the five or six years of her married life.

When she was dressed she went to the nursery, where her little boy ran to meet her, begging her to take him with her wherever she was going.

She caught him up in her arms and looked irresolutely at the imposing nurse, who was responding to his appeal in an official and determined manner, telling him that he must not cry to go in the carriage to-day; he must go for a nice walk with his nursey, because his dear papa did not like to be bothered with little boys when he was driving with his dear mamma (which was very true).

" Never mind, Alfy," said Rachel, hugging him to her maternal bosom, and covering his fair little face—which

was very like her own—with kisses;
"You shall go with mother next time,
my sweet. Don't cry, dear little man!
Suppose mother brings him home a
pretty new toy? What shall mother
bring Alfy home, nurse, eh?"

"I don't want toys, I want to go with
you, mother," wailed Alfy.

"Oh, well, I think he might," said
Rachel, weakly. "It is a fine afternoon, and he would enjoy it so! And
his father hasn't seen him for four days.
Dress him quickly, nurse, and I'll take
him. You needn't come to-day, I can
look after him quite well by myself for
once."

Alfy was accordingly dressed, his nurse
performing that operation silently, with
a mien of severe disapproval, and his

mother kneeling on the floor and helping her.

When he was ready—looking, Rachel thought, more nearly like an angel than ever child looked before—he was carried downstairs in her own caressing arms, resting his curly head on her sable collar, and clasping his mites of hands round her white throat; and she placed him in the carriage beside her, and tucked up his little legs in the soft bearskin, and they set forth together to Spencer Street in a state of beatific satisfaction and enjoyment, slightly qualified by Rachel's well-founded apprehension that her husband would scold her for spoiling the child and making a nursemaid of herself.

When Mr. Kingston arrived at the

station, closely muffled in overcoat and
comforters, it was evident to Rachel's
experienced eye—or ear rather, for as she
knew he would object to her waiting
unattended on the platform, she stayed
in the carriage and sent the footman
to meet him at the train and to take
his baggage, and so heard him before
she saw him—that he was in anything
but a good temper.

He rated an unfortunate porter who
drove a barrow in his way in un-
necessarily violent terms, and then he
demanded angrily of his servant why
the dickens they hadn't brought the
brougham for him on such a bitter day.

" Oh, Graham," said Rachel, stretching
out her hand, " how do you do, dear? I
am so sorry !—but I thought you would

like the open carriage best. It was beautifully mild when we started—it has been quite a warm day. And here is Alfy come to meet you. He is quite well, again, you see, and such a good little boy, aren't you, Alfy? He is taking care of his mother to day, and sitting so quietly."

"Why did you bring him out in the cold?" responded the father snappishly. "And where's the nurse? At home? Upon my word, Rachel, we might as well be spared the expense of servants altogether, for all the use you make of them. No, I won't kiss him—I might give him a sore throat."

"Have you a sore throat, dear?" inquired Rachel meekly, tucking the child into her own corner of the carriage, and whispering to him to sit very still.

50—2

" I should rather say so—not so much a
sore throat, perhaps, as a general bad cold
—the most confounded bad cold I ever
had in my life. I'm regularly seedy and
done up," grumbled Mr. Kingston, climb-
ing into his seat beside her.

" Oh, dear, I'm so sorry !"

" That is why I have come home to-
day," he added. " It's the most wretched
thing to be in other people's houses when
you don't feel well."

" Indeed it is," assented Rachel sympa-
thetically ; "and I am very glad you came
back. How did you catch it, do you
think ?"

" I think I must have got it before I
started. But that idiot Lambert sent
an open trap to meet me—you know
what a pouring wet day it turned out ?

—and I had to sit and be soaked for an hour and a half. Umbrellas were no good in that rain, and there was a sharp wind, too, and before we reached the house—great, cold barrack of a place, with stingy little coal fires—fancy *coal* fires!—shows what an idiot the fellow is, and she's worse—before we got there I was thoroughly wet through, and chilled to the bone. I never was so cold in my life. I took a hot bath before I dressed for dinner, and I got Lambert to send me up some brandy, but it was no use—it seemed to have regularly struck into me. I *couldn't* get warm—not till about the middle of the night, and then I felt as if I'd got a fever. I believe I have too."

" Oh, Graham, I hope not."

"It has settled on my chest," he went
on. "I haven't been able to sleep for
coughing—you know I have never had
a cough in my life—and I can't draw
a breath without feeling as if I was
dragging something up by the roots.
Can't you hear how I breathe? You
never heard me breathe like that before
did you?"

Rachel turned her blooming face, now
grave and anxious, to listen to his re-
spiration, which certainly was strangely
quick and laboured, and noisy, and she
was struck by a great change in *his*
since she had seen it four days ago.
It had become all at once wrinkled,
and hollow, and haggard—the face of
an old man.

"Oh, my dear," she exclaimed, in an

accent of genuine distress, " you *have*
got a bad cold, indeed ! Hadn't you
better call on the doctor at once -- it
won't be much out of our way—and
see what he says about it ? It may be
nothing, but I think it seems like bron-
chitis, and it is best to be on the safe side."

"I think I will," said Mr. Kingston,
covering his mouth with his wraps
again. " It seems worse than it was
when I started—the cold day, I suppose.
Hang it, I wish you had brought the
brougham—it is colder than ever !"

And he shivered under an accumulation
of great-coats and furs that one would
have thought sufficient for the temperature of polar regions.

The carriage was stopped in Collins
Street, and remained in the doctors'

quarter until little Alfy fell asleep, and
was temporarily put to bed under the
long, soft skirt of his mother's jacket.
Then, as the dusk was falling, Mr.
Kingston came back to his place, and
tremulously commanded the coachman
to drive home as fast as he possibly could.

"He says it is inflammation of the
lungs, Rachel," he whispered excitedly,
"and that I must go to bed at once.
Only a touch he called it, but he didn't
look as if he thought it a touch. He
is coming up to-night to do something.
He says I ought to have come home
the first day, and not have let it run
on. Inflammation of the lungs—that
is a dreadful thing, isn't it? I have
never had it, but I have heard of it—
it's a most dangerous complaint!"

"Oh, no, dear, not dangerous, except when people are careless," said Rachel soothingly, taking his hand under the fur rug and clasping it between her own. "And now you are home, with me to nurse you, you will soon get all right. Many people have it slightly —it is quite a common thing with a bad cold—but when they are well nursed and taken care of, they soon get all right again.

"Good little woman! you will take care of me, I know."

"Indeed I will," she responded, slipping up one hand under his arm, and resting her cheek on his coat-sleeve. "I wish you had come back to me before. But, once I get you fairly into my hands, I'll soon nurse you round."

However, though she did all that a woman and a wife, and one born to be the genius of a sick room, could do, she did not nurse him round. By the time he reached home, where the household was thrown into a panic of consternation, he was very ill indeed—his fright about himself helping very much to develop the bad symptoms rapidly; and the doctor, who next day summoned other doctors in consultation upon the case, pronounced him—not in words, but by unmistakable signs—to be in a serious and critical condition. The attack had been severe from the first; it had been allowed to run on for several days; and the constitution of the patient, enervated and shattered by years of unwholesome indulgence, was as little fitted to stand an illness as any constitution could be. The pain in breathing grew worse and worse, and the fever hotter and drier; and then stupor came on, and delirium, and exhaustion, and by and bye a filmy cloud over the sunken eyes, and a dusky pallor over the old, old, wrinkled face; and, in spite of all the doctors, and all the nurses, and all that money could do —in spite of the agonised devotion of his young wife, who never left him for more than five minutes at a time, taking snatches of sleep only when he slept, sitting by the bedside, and resting her tired head on the same pillow that she smoothed for his—it was over in less than a week. And a little paragraph appeared in " The Argus" one morning, to shock that small world of which he had so long been a distinguished ornament, with the incomprehensible intelligence that he was "gone," and would never be seen at a club mess or in a festive drawing-room again.

On the night of his death, when fever and pain and restlessness were sinking away with the sinking pulse, and when Rachel, watching beside him, thought he was past knowing anyone—even her—he looked at her with a gleam of loving recognition. "Good little woman!" he muttered in a struggling whisper. "Dear, good little woman!"

She stooped over him at once with a yearning passion of pity and vague remorse, and kissed him, and laid her white arms about him, raining tears on his dying face and his cold limp hands.

"Oh, Graham, Graham, I have not been good enough to you!" she cried. "And you have been so good—so kind—to me!"

He continued to look at her with dull wistful, pathetic eyes.

"Have I?" he gasped, feebly. "Have I?"

And then the gleam died out of his face in the shrouding darkness that was creeping over him. He was quiet for several minutes, and Rachel laid her cheek on the pillow beside him, and listened to the faint rattle which now and then told that the "step or two dubious of twilight" between sleep and death was not yet crossed, motioning the other watchers away from the bed-side, that he and she might be alone together.

And suddenly he roused himself, and said—panting the words out slowly and huskily, but evidently with a perfect consciousness of their meaning —"Rachel—you can—have him—now."

Her arm was under his pillow, and she drew it back to her gently until his head lay next her breast.

"Hush—hush—hush!" she said, with choking sobs. But he went on steadily, as if he had not heard her.

"Only tell him—not to—not to—lead little Alfy—into bad ways."

After a pause, he said,

"Do you hear!—tell him—"

"He will not—he could not!" she broke out eagerly. "He is a good, good man, though people think he is not! He will take care of little Alfy, my darling—do not be afraid—he will never lead him into bad ways—never never!"

Ought she to have said it? Had she given him—she, who, at this moment, would have laid down her life to save his, if that had been possible—the comfort she had meant to give, or a most cruel, cruel stab, in his last conscious hour? She looked at him with agonised, imploring face, which mutely prayed him to try and understand her; and there came slowly into his sunken eyes a vague intelligence and a dim, dim smile. He *did* understand her—

better, perhaps, than he had ever understood her before.

"Good little woman!" he murmured.
"Good little girl—to tell the truth."

# CHAPTER X.

### FULFILMENT.

RACHEL, who could not have dissembled if she had tried, appeared to be overwhelmed by Mr. Kingston's sudden death.

She wept herself ill, sitting now in his library chair, now in his office, now in his dressing-room, with mementoes of his domestic occupations and the homely companionship of nearly half-a-dozen wedded years around her; missing him from his accustomed place with a sense of having lost one of the best and kindest husbands that ever ungrateful woman had.

She allowed no one to touch his clothes and trinkets, or his books and pipes, or anything that he had used and cared for, but herself; and she cried over them, and kissed them, and laid them away in sacred drawers, to be treasured relics and heirlooms for her little Alfy, who was to be taught to reverence the memory of the tenderest of fathers, and to hand down to unborn generations the name and fame of the most accomplished and estimable of men.

She wandered about her great, silent house, in and out of the spacious rooms, making loving inventories of all the rich appointments, which had never had so much grace and beauty as now.

" He built this lovely place for *me*," she would say to herself, or perhaps say aloud to Beatrice, who was her chief companion at this time, " He had this carved dado made because *I* didn't like tiles ;" " he gave me this Florentine cabinet on my twentieth birthday ;" " he chose these hangings himself because he said they suited my complexion." Every bit of the house and its furniture was newly sanctified by some of these reminiscences.

She gathered together all his letters reverently—some had been waiting for his return from Mr. Lambert's, and were still unopened ; and though many of them were addressed in the kind of hand-writing that was especially calculated to arouse curiosity, she would not pry into his correspondence, nor allow anyone else to do so.

She would not read what he had evidently never intended her to read; she burnt them all without taking one of them out of its envelope, and then drove to the cemetery with a wreath of flowers for his grave.

"He was the best of husbands," she said, when to her own people she talked of him.

And Mrs. Hardy, who was truly afflicted by the family bereavement, was comforted to be able to repeat this tender formula to all the gossip of her own circle.

" He was the best of husbands. So fond of her to the last! Even when he was delirious you could see plainly his distress when she went out of the room, and his relief when she came back again. And she was so devoted! Such a thoroughly suitable marriage in every way—as if they had been made for each other! She is broken-hearted for the loss of him. And how *he* valued *her* he has plainly proved."

And here the gossips would smile decorously, and shake their heads, and say, " Yes, indeed." For they all understood what this allusion meant. It meant that Mr. Kingston had left the half of his great property absolutely at his young wife's disposal, and that she was the sole and unrestricted trustee of the rest,

which was settled upon his son; which
certainly *did* prove that he had valued
her in the most conclusive manner.

But in a little while—a scandalously
little while —indications that this young
widow of twenty-five was not incon-
solable for the loss of her elderly husband,
became apparent to all but the most
superficial observers.

It was not that she wore such very
slight mourning—soft black silks and
cashmeres that were the merest apology
for weeds—for everybody knew that
Mr. Kingston had had a horror of crape,
and had been repeatedly heard to declare
that no wife of his should wear it if
he could help it.

Mrs. Hardy had explained that it was
in deference to his wishes that she had

defied custom in this respect; and, though there was a strong impression that she ought to have insisted on paying proper respect to his memory, in spite of him—and even that his protests against conventional suttee were never intended to include this particular case (as was very probable), but only indicated his personal distaste for harsh and un-becoming materials in ladies' apparel—the fact that it was growing the fashion to be lax and independent in these matters, saved her the verdict of the majority.

And it was not that she drove about, within two months of his death, with her veil turned back over her bonnet —in the case of a veil so transparent, it didn't make much difference whether it were up or down—leaving her youthful, lovely, rose-leaf face exposed to public view as heretofore.

It was not that she was heartless or unfeeling, or that she infringed the laws of good breeding and good taste in any distinctly and visible manner.

No one could quite say what it was, and yet everyone felt that the fact was sufficiently indicated that she was recovering from the shock of her sudden and terrible bereavement with unexpected, if not unbecoming, rapidity.

"You mark my words," somebody would say to somebody else, when Mrs. Kingston's carriage went flashing by, and she turned to bow to them, perhaps with her serene, sweet, grave smile; "you mark my words—that woman will be married again by this time next year. I don't know what makes me think so, but I am sure of it. There is a look in her face as if she were going to make herself happy."

The person addressed, being a man, would probably reply that the odd thing would be if she *did* not make herself happy (and generally he suggested that by remaining a widow she would be most likely to secure that object), with youth and beauty, leisure and liberty, and ten thousand a year to do what she liked with; and that he sincerely hoped she would be.

Being a woman, she was more likely than not to look after Rachel and her carriage with solemn severity, and wonder

how it was that that poor, dear, foolish
man never could see that the girl cared
nothing at all about him, and had only
married him for his money.

Mrs. Hardy was becoming aware of
this state of public opinion with respect
to her niece's conduct—which had been
so extremely proper hitherto—and was
herself conscious of the subtle change
that had taken place, and was
uneasily wondering what it indicated,
when one day Rachel came to see
her.

It was eleven o'clock on a warm
snmmer morning, just before Christmas;
and the young widow walked over
through the gardens and the back gate,
wearing a light, black cambric dress
and a shady straw hat, looking—Mrs.

Hardy thought, glancing up at her from her writing-table in a cool corner of the now transformed drawing-room— unusually well and strikingly young and girlish.

"Well, my dear, how are you? And where's Alfy? Have you not brought him with you?"

Rachel put her arm over her aunt's shoulder, and kissed her affectionately.

"I haven't brought him to-day, because I wanted to have a little quiet talk," she said. "Are you very busy, auntie?"

Mrs. Hardy *was* busy—she always was, from breakfast until lunch time; but she was impressed by a certain gentle gravity in Rachel's voice and manner, and understood that there was something of importance to be attended to. So she gathered up her papers, told her visitor to take off her hat and sit down, and inquired anxiously what was the matter.

"There is nothing the matter," said Rachel, with a little hesitation. "But, auntie dear, I am going to—do something, and I would not do it without telling you first."

She sat upon the edge of a chair, and leaned her arms on a corner of the writing-table; and she looked into the elder woman's face with wistful, longing, pleading eyes.

Mrs. Hardy had faint, instinctive premonitions.

"Well, my dear," she replied a little brusquely, "I shall be glad to advise

you to the best of my power. But you
are your own mistress now, you know."
Then after a little pause, she said
anxiously, "What is it you are going
to do?"

"Auntie," faltered Rachel, "auntie—
you know all about Mr. Dalrymple?"

"Rachel—my *dear*—you *don't* mean to
say—! And your poor husband not six
months in his grave!"

"Not yet," said Rachel, suddenly
becoming composed and collected.
"Though I do not believe that I *ought*
to put it off. But presently, auntie—
as soon as you would think it right
—I want to marry Mr. Dalrymple. And
in the meantime he is waiting for me
to send him a message—he has asked
me to write — we want to have

the comfort of some sort of recognised engagement, if it is ever so quiet——"

"Oh, Rachel, don't ask me to have anything to do with such a thing! Only think what poor Graham would say if he could know! And he left little Alfy in your hands—and he left all that money to you—little thinking what you would do with it!"

"He knew—he knew," said Rachel. "*He* has already sanctioned it. Dear, good husband! He left me the money without any conditions if I married again, and he *knew* I should do this. It was understood between us when he died. Aunt Elizabeth, I think he wished to make reparation to Roden and me.

Don't you wish it, too? Only think, it is six years—six whole years—that poor Roden has been lonely in Queensland, without any brightness or comfort in his life; and, though he has loved me just the same, he has never attempted to do—what you would not have wished him to do—all that time. It is six years this very week, Aunt Elizabeth, since he sent Mr. Gordon down to you."

"And if he had come himself," said Mrs. Hardy, passionately, beginning to break down and cry, "I should not have let him see you—I would not have allowed you to have him. Oh, child, child! when you have grown-up daughters to look after and manage for, you will understand that I tried to

do my best for you—you will think less
hardly of me then."

Rachel jumped up from her chair,
and kneeling down flung her warm
young arms about the sobbing woman.

"My own auntie," she exclaimed
fondly, "if I could think hardly of
you I should be ashamed to live. I
*know* you tried to do your best for me
—of course I know it! It is always
a mistake to deceive people, but *I*
deceived *you*, too, not telling you all I
had done. I know you were right to
keep me away from him knowing only
what you knew. If he *had* been wicked,
as you thought, and I had had it all
my own way, what would have become
of me? But now—now that you know
he is good——"

" Ah, my dear, I don't know it!
Remember that dreadful duel! And how
can you tell that he doesn't want
you now for your money? He has
none of his own, and you have a
great fortune that he could squander
as he liked. Everyone will say
that it was for the sake of your
money."

" It would sooner have been that
the money would have kept him
from me," said Rachel softly. " Once
I was afraid of *that*. But afterwards I was ashamed that I could
have any fears. We understand
each other better. Aunt Elizabeth,
Beatrice knows that he is good—
Beatrice believes in him—and my dear
Graham gave me leave to make him

happy.    Won't    you    consent    to    it,
too ?"

" Well, if poor Graham gave you leave
it is not for me to interfere, I suppose.  But you *won't* let anyone know
you are engaged so soon ?"

" It need only be known to ourselves,
auntie."

" And you'll  promise me you won't get
married again *under* the year, at the very
earliest ?"

"Yes,  dear  Aunt  Elizabeth,  I  will
promise  you  that.    If  I  can  go  and
stay  at  Adelonga  for  a  little, and take
Alfy——"

" Is he down at the Digbys ?"

" Yes, auntie."

" Perhaps  that  will  be  the  best
plan," said Mrs. Hardy, sighing.    " It

is a quiet place, and out of the way, if only Lucilla doesn't gossip about it."

## CHAPTER XI.

### CONCLUSION.

MRS. THORNLEY was a little scandalised like her mother, at first, not by Rachel's desire to marry again—for that she should do so, as a rich young widow of twenty-five, "left" by a husband just forty years her senior, was generally anticipated as a matter of course—but by the too early announcement of those wishes and intentions which conventional decorum forbade a woman to dream of until " the year " was up.

Very speedily, however, she forgot to be shocked by anything of this kind, and devoted herself ardently to the furtherance of her cousin's happiness.

She had had Mr. Dalrymple at Adelonga after his accident, and had nursed him for about a month of his convalescence ; and since that time both she and John had had a strong feeling of friendship for him, not much less than that which they had always had for their favourite, Mrs. Digby.

They had condoned all the errors of his earlier years (even the great duel), which Mr. Gordon had assured them

was the worst episode in a reckless
but not dishonourable career, and was
in itself unstained by any mean or
vicious motives), and they had proved
the sincerity of their respect and
regard for him by allowing their son
Bruce to " chum " with him in Queensland.

And now, being put in possession of
all the facts relating to his and Rachel's
love affairs, Lucilla entered eagerly into
the arrangements which Rachel herself,
without a blush of shame, suggested for
bringing the long-parted lovers together
again.

" Oh, *yes*, my darling," she wrote hurriedly, by return of post, " pray *do*
come and spend all the summer with
us. Mamma says that as it is so *very*,

*very* soon we must be careful to keep it *quite* quiet, but John wishes me particularly to tell you that, in *his* opinion, you are *quite right*.

We both like Mr. Dalrymple *very much*, and we think he has behaved *so very well*. And John says he is not at all a spendthrift *now*, whatever he may have been *once*, and he thinks *really* that he will take care of your money and not squander it away (only he says you must let him arrange things for you on your marriage —which *must* take place at Adelonga—so as to be *quite* on the safe side); for they have had both floods and droughts *very* badly at their place in Queensland, and yet they have made it pay, which John says he *never* expected.

Bruce thinks so much of the property and the way it has been managed, that I am sure he will want to go in with Mr. Gordon if Mr. Dalrymple will let us buy him out (perhaps he *won't* now the meat-freezing is going to do such great things.) But these are details to talk of presently. We must get you here first.

If you can come on Tuesday, *do.* John will meet you at the train. I have written to Mr. Dalrymple to come the *next* day, for you must not be excited and upset until you have had time for a *good rest* after your journey. I am having the blue south room got ready for you—the one you *used* to like — and the large dressing-room next to it for dear little Alfy. *I* don't think you ought to send away your maid. Won't it *look* odd after being used to one for so long? I have *plenty* of room for her as well as for the nurse," &c., &c.

On the Tuesday, Rachel, with Alfy and his nurse, arrived, having dismissed some of her servants and put the rest on board wages, having packed up her most precious china and art treasures, and swathed her splendid upholstery in sheets of brown holland, prepared to spend any length of time at Adelonga that circumstances would admit of.

It was a beautiful day in January, rather too hot for travelling in comfort, but pleasant and breezy about the

Adelonga-hills and the bosky garden
that sheltered the old house. It was
the same old house still, Rachel was
thankful to see. Mr. Thornley had been
building with brick and stone in town,
and so had been content to leave to his
country seat, the picturesque charm of
its wooden walls and its medley of
low roofs and gables; and now it
stood embowered in cool vine leaves
and sweet-scented creepers, with great
trees of pink oleander, which loved the
sultry midsummer, nestling up against
it, and making broad splashes of sunny
colour amid the sombre richness of ever-
green shrubs—a sort of earthly paradise
in Rachel's eyes. Lucilla was standing
on the verandah, surrounded by all her
family (except her grown-up step daughter,

Isabel, who had been sent on a visit to an aunt in Sydney to be "out of the way)" waiting to greet her welcome guest; and Rachel, jumping down from the buggy, and flinging herself into those faithful arms, felt that she had been a wandering prodigal in strange countries for half a dozen years, and was on the threshold of home again.

"But, oh," she said to herself, when having seen little Alfy tucked up in his cot, and having, maidless, with her own hands, laid away her clothes in drawers and wardrobes, she began to dress for dinner, "*what* could have made Lucilla imagine that waiting for him for twenty-four hours would *rest* me?"

The long hours passed, however, as the longest hours do, and the evening of Wednesday drew on with a flaming crimson sunset; and Rachel listened for the sound of buggy wheels on distant bush tracks, and was deafened by the noise of her own loud-beating heart.

" They are coming," whispered Lucilla, creeping with the stealth of a conspirator into her cool, dim drawing-room, where the young widow stood, bright-eyed and pale, in her black gown, steadying herself with a hand on the piano.

" Shall I send him in to you by himself, dear, or would he think that was bad taste—a too open and vulgar way of recognising the state of affairs ?"

" Oh, no, he would think not it vulgar,"
replied Rachel, smiling slightly through
her air of solemn and rapt abstraction.
" You must send him by himself, Lucilla,
please—this once."

The buggy came into the garden and
passed the window. Lucilla, outside on
the verandah, welcomed her guest with
effusive inquiries after Mrs. Digby's health
and welfare, and that of all the little
Digbys' respectively; Mr. Thornley gave
loud directions to the servants about
the portmanteau that was to be carried
to the green gable room. And then the
buggy went to the stable-yard; there
was a few minutes' silence; and the
door of the drawing-room opened
quietly, and Roden Dalrymple came
in.

He had changed a little in the four years since she had seen him last; his ruddy moustache was a little more grizzled, and the lines in his sun-tanned forehead were stronger and deeper.

She was changed, too; there was a matronly grace and maturity in the roundness of her shapely figure and in the reposeful softness of her face, that had been wanting in the beauty, fresh and delicate as he remembered it, of her earlier girlish years.

But the only change they recognised in one another was their deeper capacity for understanding the worth and the meaning of such an experience as this, when, with his back against the closed door, and her hands about his neck, he

held her in both arms clasped close to
his breast, and they drank together in
one moment of speechless passion the
solace and the sweetness of all the kisses
that they *should* have had.

    \*       \*       \*       \*

In the evening Lucilla sat down to the
piano, to play some of Beethoven's
sonatas to her husband. It was a lovely
moonshiny summer night, and some of
the windows stood open, letting in the
fragrance of jessamine and tobacco,
and a quantity of tiny moths and
gnats.

Mr. Thornley, having taken his coffee
and his cigarette upon the verandah,
lying all along on a bamboo easy chair,
stayed there to listen and doze in
obscurity, with his handkerchief thrown

over his bald head to keep off the mosquitoes.

For a few minutes Mr. Dalrymple stood behind his hostess; but, finding that she played from memory, and therefore did not want leaves turned over for her, he left the piano, and crossing the room, stooped down to Rachel as she sat in a low chair dreamily fanning herself.

"Rachel," he whispered, "is the lapageria in blossom now?"

"I don't know, Roden—I don't think so," she replied.

"Shall we go and see?"

She rose at once, and they went together into the curtained alcove and through the noiseless swing door.

"Where is our seat?" he said, taking

her hand as soon as they were alone, and leading her down the dim alleys, over-arched with fern trees, and filled with broken shadows of the gigantic fronds. "I hope it is in the same place."

It was in the same place, but the place was stiller and darker than it used to be—built all round and about with gnarled masses of cork, feathered in every crevice with maiden hair, and roofed with drooping leaves.

There was just moonlight enough to enable them to find it, and when they found it they sat down side by side, and Rachel laid her head on one of her lover's broad shoulders and her hand on the other; and they remained there for several minutes without moving or speaking, listening to the far-off sound of the piano, more perfectly at rest than either of them had ever imagined it possible to be in this world.

Mr. Dalrymple spoke first, drawing a long breath.

" *Must* we be separated any more, Rachel? Can't we be married now—this week—to-morrow—and go away from everybody quietly? It seems like tempting Providence to lose sight of one another — to lose one hour more than we can help of what we have been kept out of all this time."

"It does—it does," assented Rachel. "But I promised Aunt Elizabeth that I would be a widow for a year."

"You were a widow for me—how many years?"

"I know, Roden, I know. I do not do it willingly. But other people—other things—have to be considered."

"Six months more! Child, no one has any right to demand such an enormous sacrifice of us. Who knows how long we may live to be together as we want to be together? Can we afford to throw away six months on the top of six years for the sake of mere sham propriety, knowing the worth of every hour as we do?"

"Roden," said Rachel gently, after a pause, "it shall be just as you like. If you think we ought not to wait, we will not. I can explain to Aunt Elizabeth."

And then he recognised his responsibilities.

"No," he said, "I think perhaps we had better wait—though there *is* no sense or justice in it. We'll pay Mrs. Grundy the heaviest price that she has swindled honest people of for many a day, and then we'll take it out with interest. But you will do something for me in the meantime?"

"There is nothing I could do for you that I should not want to do for myself, Roden."

"You won't go quite away, will you? You'll stay here till I have to leave, and then you'll come and stay a long while with Lily? You'll let me have sight of you, and keep watch over you, until the waiting time is up?" There was no answer required for this question. What they could do for one another they would, as both well knew. He held her tightly in his arms, covering half her face with his great moustache. "And when the time is up we will not wait one hour—not one," he said, with sudden, strong passion. "That very day, Rachel, I shall take you away to Queensland, where nobody can reach us and nothing can interfere with us. When at last I *do* get you, I will have you—for a little while at all events—absolutely and wholly to myself."

And Rachel prayed that she might be permitted to live until that "little while" should come.

It seemed, in this moment of anticipation, something that it would be presumptuous for a mortal woman to hope for, much less to expect.

\*       \*       \*       \*

And should Love, when all is said and done, be the ruler and lord of all-supreme arbiter of the destinies of purblind creatures, not one in ten, perhaps not one in fifty, of whom have the faculty to see him and know him as he is?

Should the passion of wayward girls defy the wisdom and wishes of parents and guardians, who have learned in long years of costly experience something of the potentialities of this many-sided life?

Should all risks of poverty and social ignominy, with their long train of trials and temptations, involving the welfare of innocent relatives and unborn children, be dared in an irrevocable moment of enthusiasm for one's faith in the eternal fidelity of any man or woman?

Like many other questions that trouble us in this world, wherein nothing seems quite right and nothing altogether wrong, we are constrained to leave it for the history of future ages, that we shall never see, to answer.

Knowing only what we know, we must not say "yes"—we cannot say "no." We have not sufficient light for any such generalities.

But when one finds this unique treasure of human life, to whom it is, with respect to his tangible earthly possessions, what the pearl of great price was to the merchantman of Scripture, there seems no better thing for him to do than to sell all that he has to buy it, so long as he sells only what is absolutely his own, and none of the rights and privileges that belong to other people.

THE END.